# Cardin

## Commit 7 Deadly Sins

# Compiled by Samie Sands

CW00841268

# Contents

# The Gory Greed of Gareth Gorr
## Kevin S. Hall

### Night One

I t started suddenly—unexpectedly.

Gareth had no idea how it happened—maybe he had touched the small red plant by accident? It started to affect him more and more as the minutes went past. The worst part of it was, he didn't notice until it was too late.

Gareth was 29 but he felt more like 59. He had a dead-end job at the night shift Green Sweet Centre—a piss-poor garden shop, which dealt in the weird and the strange.

Surprisingly during the day, it brought in a lot of money – but he didn't see much of it. Night shift hours were supposed to make plenty more cash, but he was on the budget end and only did a few hours a week.

He kept looking for another job but had no luck and kept getting rejection after rejection. That was... until he discovered the new red plant. Gareth was mooching around the store, tidying shelves, sweeping the floors.

It was only 2am and he was on until 8—it was going to be another long, dull night. That's when he spotted the plant in the far corner of the shop, hidden under the bottom shelf.

He would have missed it had it not been for the bright redness of it. It looked a bit like a tulip, but it had a long blue stalk and three red heads, sat in a small, dusty pot. There was no name or label on it, and there only looked to be one of them. Gareth picked it up, nicking his finger on one of the spikes on the stalk.

He had almost dropped it there and then—he had been known for his clumsiness—and swore to himself. His first instinct was to keep it for himself. It was his find after all. But then he thought if he showed it to the manager in the morning, they might display it and it might make him much more popular.

Truth be told, Gareth was a bit of a slob; not shaving, brown hair a mess, and he was a little overweight, but he still dressed sharply for work. Cool but casual was his motto. He was a little OCD about cleanliness too, so he immediately went to wash his hands. As he did this, he was unaware of the red spores that were already making their way into his bloodstream, starting to change his shape.

Gareth continued with the rest of his shift, a little more upbeat and happier about his new find, which would surely be the envy of his colleagues and make him a lot more respected around here.

Little did he realize that his luck was about to change, and that envious of the seven deadly sins, Greed, was about to take over...

## Night Two

Gareth felt a bit seedy. Nothing too major but he had been sweating as he slept during the day, and his throat was a bit dry. Not that that stopped him from turning up to work. He had apparently been the talk of the shop all day—his red plant, which he had named Garethos Plantos Red, was displayed in the front window, and business had been blooming.

He was even given a raise and the manager was most impressed with the cleanliness of the shop. Yet at night, the plant took on a sinister form. It seemed to have teeth on the stalk and the three heads were bent low, as if they were watching him.

Of course, it was surely all in his imagination. Gareth had started to become greedy already—he was due to be interviewed for the local paper, radio station and demanded more attention—the rest of the town needed to know it was him that found the plant, and him alone.

Gareth continued about the shop, whistling a merry tune, happy things were going his way. Then, about halfway through the night, the nightmare started. Two local teens broke into the shop and tried to steal the plant. Gareth heard the break of glass as he was out the back having a short break.

He grabbed what he could find...a large rake around the corner ought to scare whoever was there off. He cautiously walked around the large display shelves holding various colorful plants. Gareth recognized one of them—scruffy Dean Topps and an older kid, who had a cigarette in his mouth.

Gareth listened in angrily to their conversation, gripping the rake tighter, feeling the red spores work inside him, clenching his skin and making him sweat.

"Gareth is a creepy twat that doesn't deserve all of this," Dean said. "He's a grumpy sod at the best of times. Let's grab that plant of his and destroy it."

The other kid shook his head, smiling sickly. "I've got a better idea. Let's burn it." He laughed, getting out his lighter.

Gareth stepped out with the rake. "Right, you two assholes are in trouble now. Don't you move."

Dean took out a knife and moved forward. "Don't try anything old man, we are taking that plant."

"Old man?" Gareth gritted his teeth. "I'm 29!"

Dean lunged forward but Gareth was quicker. He shot out with the rake, only meaning to knock Dean out. But the spikes went through Dean's head, blood gushing out horribly onto the floor.

The other kid panicked and began to run, but Gareth swiped at him too, the rake slicing through the body, blood spurting everywhere.

It was over so quickly but to Gareth it had gone by so slowly. He watched as the plant's vines extended and touched the bodies, dragging them towards it as the heads opened.

Gareth could feel his body expanding as he felt the taste of flesh in his mouth, as if the spores inside him were linked to the plant, and the bodies were soon crushed into bloody paste, the plant not leaving one drop or trace. Gareth sat back, breathing heavily.

The spores were consuming him, but the terrifying thing was...he liked what was happening. He needed to feast on his greed more. He needed more flesh.

## Night Three

Gareth was sweating more and more, yet he was feeling the pleasure more than the pain. The plant had given him a hunger for human flesh and a power for wealth and fortune beyond his wildest dreams—and nightmares.

The third night was unobtrusive enough, but he had been on edge ever since those teens had been fed to the plant. It had made him tense and unable to sleep much during the day.

No one had said anything at work though, and no police had come by to see about the murders. He did the interview with the radio station but had to wear gloves—his fingers and palms were now a red color, almost pulsating, and he had grown sharp, yellow claws.

Yet his thirst for more wealth and hunger continued. Gareth had lured an unsuspecting prick from the internet who was out to expose him, and who had already ruined other people's lives for his own gain.

Gareth thought if he could get unsavory and nasty people for the plant, they wouldn't be missed as much. He stood by the plant, which was now in a bigger soil patch. He could hide any mess in there and cover it up, without anyone noticing.

Gareth gripped the large sharp spade in his hands, waiting for Lyle to appear. He tried to retain his breathing and be more relaxed. This had to go as smoothly as possible—nothing could tie it to him.

The shop bell tingled, and it was quite loud in the eerie silence.

"Gareth? It's Lyle. I'm here about the story. I can pay you big money if you let me use your plant on the front page. I just need to borrow it for a few days…"

Gareth stepped out into the light. His hair had turned red and his eyes were black as the night. He was grinning.

"Oh… I don't think so, Lyle. I know all about your sordid past. Now you are to become plant food for the greater good."

Before Lyle had a chance to react, Gareth brought the spade down hard on Lyle's head, caving it in.

Blood splattered the work area, splattered the soil, making the plant wither with excitement. Gareth kept bringing the spade down again and again, until he could feel the plant sucking the body into the earth, and he too could taste the flesh.

Gareth's neck started to creak, and green veins appeared, almost like the vines of the plant. His eyes were black, but his pupils were a sharp, staring red that didn't blink.

Lyle would serve the plant well for another night. But he noticed the heads had become larger, and the teeth more vicious. Gareth too was changing—but little did he know that his change was going to get him noticed a lot more. Greed was slowly taking over, and not for the best.

Gareth managed to clean up the mess and remove and burn his clothes. It was then he looked at his fingers and saw the sharp teeth appearing on them. What was he turning into? The trouble was, he didn't want to stop, and even though the third night was almost over, the terror was just beginning...

### Night Four

The days were all merging into one nightmare. Gareth was having terrible, awful dreams. He couldn't sleep and would only get a few minutes a day before waking in cold sweats.

His hands were now big, puffy and red; his fingers covered in sharp teeth. His hair had turned a bright red and his lips were dry. Gareth's eyes were dark with sharp, staring red pupils.

He had to wear sunglasses and a hat to work so no one could see what he looked like. Yet his greed was getting worse—his was trending on all the social platforms and his plant was getting lots of media attention—good and bad.

Gareth wanted to re-veal his secrets but knew where that would get him. Sooner or later, the three murders would catch up with him.

But for now, he wanted the fame, the fortune and the friends, even if it meant his body had to suffer as a result. Gareth was getting a little slower as he worked through his shift. The red spores were twisting his body and making him ache all over.

Yet tonight, he would find out, the plant wanted more than human flesh. Gareth was sweeping up dirt left from the previous day—straightening up the shelves as he went. He was happy now and wondering which bad guy to feed to the plant next...when he could hear whispering in his head.

It was not human. It was old, low, alien. His gaze took him over to the plant—the three red heads were bent, looking in his direction. They were almost swaying, hypnotizing him, making him come closer, and closer.

"GARETH..." The plant was speaking inside him, and its voice sent shivers down his spine. "YOU HAVE DONE WELL SO FAR. BUT WE NEED MORE. MORE SOULS FOR US TO FEAST. THEN WE WILL CONSUME YOU, SO WE CAN BE AS ONE. ONE MIND TO TAKE OVER THIS WORLD."

"I...I don't..." Gareth stammered, trying to find words.

"DON'T THINK, GARETH. JUST OBEY US. USE YOUR GREED. WE GORGE UPON IT. BRING US OUR NEXT VIC-TIM. YOUR BOSS."

"My...boss?"

"DON'T PLAY COY, GARETH. YOU KNOW WHAT HE HAS DONE. THOSE IM-AGES ON HIS LAPTOP? HE NEEDS TO PAY. BRING HIM AND WE WILL RE-WARD YOU WITH MUCH MORE."

Gareth didn't want to obey. But the plant had him in its vine grip, and his smile turned into a grin, as the plant started to take over his own voice too. He laughed as he set about bringing in his boss.

"THE EARTH WILL RUN RED TOMORROW NIGHT," he growled, sitting in the corner and rocking backwards and forwards until dawn...

### Night Five

Gareth dragged his boss's mutilated body into the shop, in a white canvas bag. His boss had been a big, fat man, and luckily no one had seen Gareth cave in his head or slice through the body, cutting up the parts to make it easier to give to the soil.

He had been a bit late for work, but nobody seemed to care now—so long as he kept his plant healthy and sales were up. Gareth also had the perfect story in case anyone wondered where his boss yet—and he had those images to give to the police should the need arise.

His plant was bending its heads again, and the opening petals seemed to be smiling at him. The vines withered with excitement as Gareth placed each of the body parts into the soil—watching them sink, slurp and grind into the soil.

As he watched sickeningly as the head was swallowed, the plant had somehow gotten bigger.

"GOOD..." he could hear the plant talking within him again. "CAN YOU FEEL MY LIFE FORCE THROUGH YOUR BODY? FEEL HOW GOOD IT IS. HOW MUCH MORE I NEED SO WE CAN BE ONE."

"Four...Four more victims and then we are done. I do not know how much longer this can go on. People will soon notice..."

"NONSENSE. I HAVE THE POWER TO HYPNOTISE THEM. DURING THE DAY, THEY ARE OBLIVOUS TO WHAT HAS HAPPENED. YOU CAN CONTINUE YOUR WORK. FEEL THE CHANGE..."

Gareth arched his back, feeling a pain shoot up it, but he didn't mind it. He could feel vines inside him, stretching and growing. His face was now red; his whole-body red.

As he grinned, his teeth were covered in earth and worms wriggled in between. He bent forward; his face up close to the plant. Its pull was strong, it was intoxicating. "I know you...I can see your world...The horror that happened. This is now your world. There will be more of your kind—I promise. We will make your race shine on this planet once again."

The plant laughed—like the chattering of a thousand teeth, sending new shivers down Gareth's back. "YOU REALLY DO SEE. THERE IS SO MUCH HORROR IN THIS WORLD. SO MUCH MISERY. BRING IT TO ME SO I CAN BE FREE."

Gareth nodded. He could feel the vines in him twist and contort his body. His neck suddenly began to stretch, and he could feel the muscles burn, the pain, but he somehow enjoyed it. The neck stretched and split in two—green vines withering in the gap, covered in sharp teeth.

Gareth's eyes glowed red, his face was turning red. As he could feel his shoulders rip open, two red, bulbous plant heads sprouted forth, gnashing their teeth and latching onto his skin.

He was transforming into one of them at a terrifyingly fast rate and was nervous someone would notice him.

Gareth had to find his next four victims fast for the cycle to be complete. His speech was becoming slurred and deep, and he spat a lot more than he used to. He wasn't even thinking of cleaning up the shop now. There were more important matters to attend to.

Like the slavery of the human race.

## Night Six

Gareth had no clue what day it was, or even who he was any more. He just craved human flesh and to be like his plant. It whispered to him dark things and its even darker plans as he tried to sleep during the day.

He wanted to sleep, to find out more and more about what was inside. He had never been a skeptical bloke—Gareth believed in the paranormal, the urban myths of the world, but he hadn't believed in visitors from other planets...until this new one.

He called him Eggg—no reason, but it was the word he heard the most during the dreams, and Gareth stuck with it. The dreams were of human/plant hybrids taking over his town, and devouring those who were bad, while turning those who were good into them.

Gareth was now looking up his next victim—a nasty piece of work who preyed on the vulnerable and poor. Lloyd had to be next.

Gareth made his way to the back of the house, making sure to stick to the shadows so no one saw him. He was slowly changing beyond recognition as a human now.

Greed had manifested itself in him and overtook him—he didn't care who he hurt as long as Eggg was fed. Gareth pick-locked the door and crept in, making his way up the stairs.

It was dark—but somehow the sharp, staring red pupils in his sunken black eyes made them infrared.

He could easily sniff out the human flesh now too, and it made him grin. His head was now twice as large and all red—almost in the shape of the flower itself.

His arms were thick, twisty vines that moved of their own accord, and his hands were puffed red, with yellow, sharp pincers for fingers. His body was bloated and stretched, yet his arms and legs were the strongest he had ever been and made

Gareth a lot faster and stronger. He carried the meat cleaver in his hands as he giggled to himself, saliva staining his mud-covered coat. He stopped outside Lloyd's room and could hear heavy breathing coming from with-in.

The plant had shown him the bad things Lloyd had done—this guy was a son of a bitch that had to be put down. Yet as Gareth listened in, something was not right. The stench in the air had changed to something else...something...alien.

It was not unlike...Gareth crashed open the door as thunder and lightning crackled outside—and he gasped, stopping in his tracks and dropped the meat cleaver.

There was Lloyd—or what used to be Lloyd—sunk into his bed, which was splattered in blood and all over the walls.

As the lightning flashed again, Gareth could make out Lloyd's face—it was like his—bulbous, large but blue, with sunken black holes and sharp white pupils.

Small, sharp incisors were where his mouth had been, and his body had shrunken and stretched. Lloyd smiled as best he could, relishing in the shock on Gareth's face.

"What, Gareth, did you think you were the only one? Eggg didn't tell you about his enemy, did he? They have been fighting for a millennia and now they are fighting for this planet. The only question is... which side are you on?"

Gareth smiled sickly and closed the door. "I choose the greedy, winning side," he grinned. This was either going to be an awfully long—or very short—bloody night.

### Night Seven

Gareth awoke, a little dazed and confused, with a banging headache. He could hear the same, heavy breathing as before, but now with a rasp to it. How long was he out for? He had to get back to Egg straight away...

"Don't worry," a deep, raspy voice said. He knew it was Lloyd though.

"It's only been a day. You are still here. When you were knocked out, I went to get your plant. My, my, he's certainly grown a lot, hasn't he? Must be all that human flesh..."

"I...I only killed the bad. I had to—to keep us both alive!"

Lloyd nodded, sympathetically. "I was the same with Eggg at first. Until all he wanted was to consume flesh and be the best—greedy, selfish, only wanting one thing—to take over this world. I... put a stop to him.

You can do the same to Eggg too—before it's too late for you."

Gareth shook his head. "It can't be true. Eggg wants to make us equal—humans and his kind living together, working together..."

Lloyd scoffed. "Don't be absurd. They are planet killers—conquerors, only thinking of themselves. The horror, the terror I have seen..."

"You're lying," Gareth said, through gritted teeth. "Eggg would never betray us. He is here to save us!"

Gareth lunged for Lloyd, who swiped out with his bulbous blue hands and sharp claws, knocking Gareth to the floor, causing a massive gash on his head.

Surprisingly, Gareth could not feel a thing, and felt stronger than he ever had. He sat up and spotted something behind Lloyd.

It was Eggg, who had grown immensely since Gareth last saw him. The plant's body was also swirling red, almost hypnotizing him. Eggg's three heads were swaying and merging into a giant one, with sharp teeth forming as the mouth opened wider.

Gareth saw his chance—he kicked out at Lloyd, knocking him backwards to-wards the plant. Lloyd turned around but it was too late—the plants giant mouth chomped down onto Lloyd's head, blood gushing everywhere, splattering the walls, floor and bed.

Gareth had to look away, as the slurping and crunching sound became too much. When the noises stopped, he looked back. Eggg was not there, although there was a pool of blood there were Lloyd had been.

Gareth shook his head, no idea what was going on. It was then he heard Eggg's voice inside him again, and the grim reality was becoming all too clear.

"Yes...feel my energy through you. I am still at the shop, Gareth. This was all you. You ate Lloyd and you are becoming more and more like me. Feel the flesh and blood inside you? Consume that greed. It is all you crave."

Gareth wanted to hate himself and end this—but for the most part he took great pleasure in the kills. After all—he was only killing the wicked and cruel. Eggg was slowly replacing his human side, and soon, only Eggg would remain.

He licked the blood from his fingers and went about cleaning up the room – it would be so Lloyd had never existed.

The next night was to be the most nightmarish and intense yet, but Gareth knew what had to be done. For the greater good.

## Night Eight

Gareth awoke and went into work as normal. The last week almost seemed like a fever dream—a nightmare he couldn't escape.

But for the first night in a long time, he felt refreshed—energized for the work ahead. He had almost forgotten the night before...until he saw Eggg in the window, glaring at him with his now one giant head.

It was almost hypnotic the way the plant swayed like that, its thick, curled green vines for its body withering, the sharp teeth on its mouth in the shape of a sick grin. It knew what it was doing, and this angered Gareth even more.

Greed it seemed, had taken over, and as Gareth entered the shop, chills ran up his body. The shop was in disrepair—shelves were smashed, plants strewn every-where, the tills and back were covered in mud...but that was far from the worst.

Several mutilated bodies lay across the floor. Some with body parts missing, others flesh ripped off and insides splashed across the white marble panels, the red sickly bright from the lights of the shop.

He gingerly made his way towards the plant, anger more than fear taking over him. Gareth fought the urge to reach out and grab the plant, ripping it to shreds. His fists clenched, as he stared into the teeth.

"Why... why do this?" Eggg's hollow, long laugh sent chills down his spine.

"It wasn't me. It was you; don't you remember? We needed those other victims quickly and you were hungry after all. Your body is strong enough now to handle all that meat. Soon I will completely consume you and make you mine forever."

Gareth gritted his teeth. "I thought we were working together—so your race can co-exist with the human race?"

"I need a human host to survive. That first night I planted my seeds inside you—my children could taste the flesh and be free—then they can birth and search for new hosts. The cleansing will now begin!"

Gareth shook his head, unsure of what Eggg was meaning...until he felt the excruciating pain coming from his throat and back.

He stumbled backwards, falling on-to one of the broken shelves. Little by little, the flesh on his neck popped and three small plants slithered out. The same happened on his back and two more ripped from his stomach.

Five altogether—small, baby versions of Eggg, who all moved towards their mother.

"You were the perfect host for my children to be born. I just needed to keep you until the time was right. After this you will slowly start to die from the poison in your body—and my children will find new hosts to infect. As you once said, this planet is filled with evil – a perfect playground for my kind!"

Gareth tried to regain control—he could feel the blood leave his body, but the poi-son was already beginning to take over.

"I...I will find a way to beat you."

"It's too late," Eggg chuckled. "More of my kind are on the way as I speak—flower shops and homes up and down the world will soon know and fear us."

Gareth looked out of the window, and to his amazement, saw what looked like red streaking comets shoot from the sky and to the world below.

Then, one simple, greedy thought overcame him and it was the only way to stop Eggg for good...

### Night Nine

The days and nights all seemed to be meshing into one. Gareth wasn't sure what was real and what wasn't anymore, but one thing was clear—Eggg had to be destroyed.

For all the greed, deaths and heartache he had gone through, this would surely be the only decent thing left in his human part of the brain to do.

The night was dark and full of terrors, as someone once said.

Gareth opened the door to the shop. He had no idea how he had gotten home or why he was still alive. Surely Eggg would catch on and learn of his plan? Then he shook the notion from himself.

No...he could not let the plant know what was about to happen. As much as it disgusted him to do so, this was the only way. He went to where the plant was sleeping—or dozing...or was it pretending to lower its head like a crocodile, ready to pounce when the prey got near?

Gareth was almost plant-like now—most of his human features had gone. Only his now small eyes were wide and staring, and he could see perfectly in the dark.

He did not switch on the lights and made as little sound as possible. Gareth started on the vines—ripping them apart and devouring them.

It partly tasted human, partly something else...a sensation that almost made him gag and one not from this Earth.

But he had to continue.

He started on the plants base, munching and crunching the soil it was sat in, determined not to leave a trace behind. It was then that Eggg woke up.

"Gareth? No! What are you doing? This was not our plan! Stop! I could make you king! The greediest, fattest king this world has ever seen!"

Gareth ignored the plant and started towards the head, pushing it down so the teeth wouldn't snap and try to swallow him whole.

He bit down hard on the large bulbous head, black, red and green goo spraying out and all over the place and all over Gareth. His gaze was fiery, fierce, intense.

The plant let out a blood-curdling scream that was far from human. Gareth pushed down harder as he tore through the head with his teeth, ripping off chunks and swallowing them hard.

It was done.

Gareth slumped back against the side of the wall, shivering all over. He noticed the baby plants, but without their mother, they were shriveling up and dying. He did not know about the other plants out there now—but he had a sense that without a queen they would be lost, and the humans would prevail.

It was their planet after all, and they would defend it to the last. Gareth spent most of the night disposing the bodies, trying to salvage much of the plants as he could, and making the place look as good as it could possibly be.

To his surprise, there hadn't been too much damage than he first feared. As Gareth felt a weight off his shoulders, he had no clue that there was one more final terror to come, and it was not truly over.

The sky outside was now pulsating green and red, and he had no idea what time of day it was. A monstrous shadow spilled onto the shop—much larger than what Eggg had been and envisioned to him.

Gareth knew this wasn't going to be as easy. But then he had a plan. One final, greedy, nasty plan that might just stop this forever.

Ten.

It didn't matter if it was day or night now. Gareth had to clear his mind and concentrate on all the other plants out there. They had to follow his thoughts and converge on the gigantic plant stomping through his town, teeth gnashing and huge purple head trying to get into other human's minds.

Gareth put his hands to his temples and closed his eyes—he could see the other plants about to strike the humans, but with immense thought and strength both Lloyd and Eggg had given him, he was able to get them to turn around and head in the direction of this new monstrosity.

The thing was almost at his door—each stomp it made on the ground felt like a million earthquakes—and the roars it made were deafening. Gareth swung open the door and looked up at the towering plant.

So, this must be the queen. Eggg could have been one of her generals—maybe even second-in-command, and now she was dead, the queen would be pissed.

Gareth grinned as the queen looked down on him. "Oh bitch, you have no idea what's coming do you? When I consumed Eggg I got her powers too and knew your weaknesses. Do no harm on each other? Well, I have news for you..."

The queen looked down in horror, as all the plants were ascending her, and started to bite into her, tearing her to shreds. They were crawling and swarming all over her, like flies on jam.

Gareth smiled. "Oh yeah—I just happened to pass on my greed and despair onto them as well. They know what humans can be capable of and knew they couldn't win. All it took was to eat one of your own to learn more. Now my last sight is the sight of you failing. Humanity will prevail again."

The queen was helpless to stop as Gareth took out a gun and, without hesitating, blew his head off.

Blood splattered the ground as the queen toppled over, crashing to the ground and the plants finishing off on her flesh. Most of them were dying, but a few of them managed to escape back into the sky and out into the solar system, looking for another planet to feast on.

Without a leader though, most would not make it. As the skies cleared and returned blue, baffled authorities and witnesses tried to cover it up the best they could, to avoid mass panic and the wider world finding out.

But unknown to most, some of Gareth's blood had seeped into the shop and into one of the baby plants lying beside the door.

The blood consumed it and it started to twitch, coming to life and the head rising, vines twitching with excitement. It grinned as it watched the humans go about their business. It would bide its time—but the shop would be rebuilt and there would be plenty more Gareth's in this world.

There was plenty of greed in humans and this was far from over.

THE END?...

# Kevin S. Hall

Kevin Hall is 35 and lives in Haddington, East Lothian in Scotland. He is a sci-fi, fantasy and horror fan, his biggest loves being Stephen King and Doctor Who. He has written Thirteen: A Collection Of Horror Stories, and Thirteen Vol. 2: The Horror Continues and is beavering away on Vol. 3: The Never-Ending Horror at the moment.

He is currently writing his first full horror novel Ravens Edge, and is working on several anthologies - a High Fliers superhero one, a fantasy one and a Halloween one. Submissions are always welcome for short stories too. In his spare time, he loves to read, is doing a Games Designer Course, and does a Radio Show on a Sunday on Radio Saltire too.

# A Few Imperfections
# Thomas M. Malafarina

*"There is a kind of beauty in imperfection."* - Conrad Hall

"Things are beautiful if you love them." - Jean Anouilh

"In our world of readily available cosmetic surgery, it is possible that an attractive couple could end up having an ugly baby and not understand why." - Thomas M. Malafarina

The young, obviously wealthy couple drove along the winding country road at a speed much faster than they should have been driving. Despite the fact that their Lexus LS 460 with its $80,000 price tag was equipped to handle the curves; they were still traveling at too high of a speed. This was probably the result of the intense discussion going on inside the vehicle; one that was rapidly degenerating into a full-blown argument.

"What in the hell are we supposed to do, Stephen?" Angela asked, genuinely concerned.

"What do you mean?" Stephen asked feigning ignorance yet knowing exactly what she was talking about. It was all she had been talking about since they got in the car after leaving the hospital. Tucked away in the back seat of the sedan, safely secured in his car seat, their newborn baby boy, Stephen Thurston Wellington III cooed to himself, oblivious to the conversation, which was taking place in the front of the car or the fact that he was the subject of that conversation.

"You know exactly what I mean. What are we going to do about... the baby... and his... appearance?"

"Angela, please. I don't understand what you're getting so upset about. He's only two days old for God's sake." Stephen said trying to look at the situation rationally and simultaneously calm his wife down. However, he knew his effort was likely wasted, since once Angela got an idea in her head nothing could stop her from venting.

"But... but he's... he's hideous Stephen. There... I've... I've finally said it aloud. And don't tell me you haven't been thinking the exact same thing. I saw the way you looked at him."

"Jesus Angela. That's an incredibly horrible and thoughtless thing to say about your own child. My God... how could you even think such a thing let alone express it?"

"I know... and I feel terrible saying it but for Christ's sake Stephen. Somebody has to address the ugly elephant in the room. You have to agree with me Stephen. He's... he's heinous."

"Now I wouldn't say anything as drastic as that, Angela. He might be a bit odd looking, maybe even a tad on the funny-looking side but all newborns are less than attractive than they should be, with their wrinkly pink skin, and pinched faces. It's perfectly normal. I'm sure he'll look better as he grows. I'll admit he has a few imperfections, but I'm sure we'll get used to them."

"No... no I don't think I can Stephen. I think there is something very wrong with him... with little Stephen's looks. I mean how in the world could two people as good looking as we are manage to create such an atrocious looking little child? You know we're both very attractive Stephen... I don't think it vain to admit such a thing, do you?"

"No. I suppose not." Stephen replied, not certain he agreed. He knew what she said about them however was true. They were both quite attractive.

"Maybe there was a mix-up at the hospital. Maybe they gave us some ugly couple's baby and they got our baby by mistake. Do you think that's possible Stephen?"

"No... I don't. They have all sorts of safeguard in place for that kind of thing. Besides, we both saw him being born. We saw him the second he took his first breath. That's our baby Angela. Now getting back to your original question about how we could have a... less than attractive child. If you I think about it, the only reason we're both so good looking is that we can afford to look so good. Our parents were both wealthy and we were only children so fixing our imperfections wasn't a big deal for them. After they died, we inherited all of their money. We also earn good incomes on our own. We eat well, we go to the gym, we pamper ourselves at spas and we generally take good care of ourselves. Also as you may recall when we met a few years ago, you had told me you had some work done over the years before we knew each other."

"Yes I did mention I had a few minor alterations. And you admitted to having some cosmetic work done yourself, didn't you?"

"I did. But now that I think about it, I don't believe we ever discussed what sorts of procedures we had done. Perhaps that's something we should have discussed."

"Maybe you're right, Stephen. Perhaps we should have. I mean it's not really a big deal. When I was a pre-teen, I had a severe overbite and my parents got me braces to straighten out my teeth. If I remember correctly you had braces as well didn't you?"

"Yes... as did most the boys in my boarding school. My teeth were quite twisted and a bit gnarly, but the braces and a few orthodontic surgeries took care of that. And we both have poor eyesight and have had laser to correct our vision issues so we don't have to wear glasses. When I was about ten I also had a minor surgery to correct a muscular issue with my left eye that caused it to turn inward sometimes."

"Well... that explains a lot." Angela said with sudden realization, "I think little Stephen might have that same eye thing."

Stephen shot back, "What do you mean? He can't even see yet! His eyes don't have the ability to focus, that's why they seem to roam all over the place. Seriously, are you going to try to blame me for all of this?

We made this child together Angela. He was created from genes from both of us. So tell me... what else have you have done that I don't know about?"

"As I told you, it was all minor and insignificant things. For example, my nose was a bit wide and I had it thinned out a bit several years ago. I also just recalled something else I had forgotten about. When I was about four, my ears stuck out and my mother took me to a doctor who pinned them back for a while until they stayed back on their own."

"Our baby's ears stick way out." Stephen added, "In fact, he looks like a taxi cab driving down the highway with its both doors hanging open. And he has a funny-looking wide nose. So those deformities obviously must have come from you."

"Yeah? Well what about that weak chin of his. He barely has any chin at all. His mouth hangs open in a hangdog fashion that makes him look half-retarded. I think he got that from you Stephen. Tell me... was that jutting masculine Hollywood leading man chin of yours with you since birth or did you have it modified?"

Stephen hesitated for a moment then admitted, "Ok. I might have not had much of a chin when I was younger and may have had minor implant surgery to enhance it, but my chin issues were not as severe as the baby's."

"Ah ha!" Angela shouted, "Another flaw of yours, which apparently was destined to curse our poor malformed baby." She took off her seat belt and turned around to try to examine the baby closer. But she was unable to see him tucked away as he was in his car seat.

"Angela, for the last time, he's not malformed, he just has a few imperfections. And since we're pointing out those imperfections, what about that unibrow of his? No one in my family ever had any such thing. As I recall from pictures of your Dad when he was alive, he had quite the crop of eyebrow foliage. Tell me Angela, did you inherit that and maybe have it surgically removed as well?"

"I... I... I might have once had a bit more hair between my brows than I would have cared for and maybe I did have it removed with a bit of laser work."

"So... you are the one responsible for that wooly caterpillar crawling across my baby's eyebrows after all."

"But what about his big bulging eyes. My eyes are normal and they always have been. You're the one with the protruding mooneyes... Dear!" Angela said sarcastically.

"Mooneyes? You used to call them 'large luminous pools of emotion'. Now you call them mooneyes? Why don't you just call them bug eyes as long as you're being so nasty? And to make matters worse you think my eyes are ugly on our baby! I really don't get you Angela."

"Yeah well maybe we should have had this discussion before we decided to create that little cave troll in the back seat!"

"Cave troll? Honest to God Angela! I can't believe you could say such a thing about your own flesh and blood. You're nothing but a self-centered cow!" Steven was now staring daggers at Angela feeling like he was speaking with some horrible creature he had never met before.

"Oh just wonderful! Make fun of my additional weight after I just gave birth to your little freak."

Stephen was furious. For the first time in his married life, he felt like reaching over and punching his wife right in the face. As a result, he took his eyes off the highway for just a few seconds too long. As he approached a curve in the road, a large buck strolled lazily out of the woods and onto the roadway and right in his path.

"Look out Stephen!" Angela screamed.

Stephen did the one thing he should never have done and that was he swerved to avoid hitting the beast. He quickly lost control of his sedan and skidded off the highway, down a steep embankment and full-bore right into a giant clump of trees.

The front of their sedan slammed into a huge tree and one of its broken branches crashed through the windshield and pierced Stephen's heart killing him instantly. His corpse was pinned behind the wheel as last of his blood spurted from his chest and trickled from his mouth and down his chin. A split second later Angela, who had not refastened her seat belt flew through the windshield and became impaled on several other remnants of branches. She unfortunately took several minutes to die as she hung pierced and screaming in agony. The last sound she heard, as her lifeblood pumped from her body were the cries of her ugly baby apparently still safe and unharmed secured in his car seat.

Several hours later the rescue workers had successfully removed both of the corpses from the scene and had gotten the baby out of the back seat of the sedan. One of the Emergency Medical Technicians was a young woman named Naomi Jacobson. She was holding the baby and rocking it after having determined the boy was uninjured. Naomi was a short stocky woman who at first glance one might consider a bit unattractive if not somewhat homely. She was however, happily married to an equally stout man and less than attractive man who owned a plumbing business.

The two had been unable to conceive and had been on a waiting list for possible adoption for many years, yet to date they had been unsuccessful. Naomi wanted a baby more than anything else in the world. She looked down at the wrinkled little boy with his odd-looking nose, unibrow, slightly twisted mouth and ears which stuck outward and she fell instantly in love. She thought he was the most beautiful baby she had ever seen. Sure, he had a few imperfections, but who didn't? She decided she would speak with the agent from Child's Services when she arrived, and tell her she would love to be able to adopt this baby if by some chance there were no living relatives to claim the child. Unknown to Naomi at that time her wish would come true.

# Thomas M. Malafarina

Thomas M. Malafarina is a horror fiction author from the South Heidelberg Twp area of Berks County, Pennsylvania. He was born July 23, 1955, in Ashland, Schuylkill County, PA where he lived until moving to Berks County in 1979.

Many of Thomas's stories take place in his native Schuylkill County and also in Berks County settings. Thomas's books are published by Sunbury Press of Mechanicsburg, PA.

Thomas's early novels included 99 Souls, Burn Phone and Eye Contact all three of which are now out of print, having been reworked and re-titled by Thomas from 2016-2018. They were replaced by the new books, It Waits Below, Burner and From the Dark. His novel, Fallen Stones is currently still available although this also is being reworked by Thomas and will eventually be called Circle of Blood and re-released. Other novels include three in his Dead Kill series, Dead Kill Book 1: The Ridge Of Death, Dead Kill Book 2: The Ridge of Change and the third installment, Dead Kill Book 3: The Ridge of War.

# Fountain's Wish
## Lachelle Redd

Jonathan Fountain emerged from a deep sleep that Saturday. The week proved successful and now his workout would complete the process. With a sprawling 3,000 square foot home complete with the finest gym equipment money could buy, Jonathan preferred showing off at the local gym. The pride he took in being fit ranged somewhere in between healthy and deranged. Raw eggs, protein shakes, special diets, you name it, he tried it. The man lived for the two to three-hour workouts and craved the results afterwards. Jonathan obsessed about his appearance. The man had mirrors in every room and a pose for each.

Fountain zipped through town in his dark blue Jeep Rubicon. With the top off, the man wanted the world to admire everything about him. The job, the status, the physique, the thousands of dollars spent on capped teeth and hair restoration made a complete package of vanity and self-adoration. But today would bring about a new phase.

Fountain whipped into the parking lot at the local gym and into a space that allowed a full visual through the reflection in the glass floor to ceiling glass window. He strolled across the parking lot checking his Fitbit and slyly watching for an audience. A group of young girls giggled and flirted as he strolled by. Of course, he returned the favor. They were young, legal and willing to bend to his will. At least, that was the way he wanted things.

"Ladies, when I'm done here, maybe one of you can escort me to my truck and dinner. I can always leave it up to you to decide, but that's not my game. Who wants to play?"

Of the four women in the group, only one stepped forward. The others lost interest. The over macho attitude immediately killed the vibe, but the one who remained moved eagerly into his web.

"I'll take you up on that offer and promise you, I play like no one you've ever bedded."

Jonathan's wicked smile and beautiful brown eyes twinkled. For him, she would be a weekend thing, something to play with until Monday. But for her, it would be so much more.

"I have to get my workout in. You can wait for me or just come back in two hours or so."

The beautiful woman had already figured him out and spoke without haste.

"Actually, I just got here. I have to get my workout in. So, you do you and I will work on me. Deal?"

Intrigued by her response, Jonathan gave the woman a quick nod.

"Sounds good to me. I'll stay out of your way. And by the way, the name's Jonathan."

"I'm Ginn." She strolled to the door and waited.

Pleased with the woman's response, Jonathan held the door open and watched her ass as she sauntered by. He felt pride in the new conquest and visually placed the woman in his bed.

In the hours that followed, Jonathan's workout presented with more grunts and groans as he tried to gain Ginn's attention. The attorney applied heavier weights to boost the difficulty of the workout not to mention the peacock like strut to garner her attention. Neither worked, Ginn continued her routine without a second thought of the show playing out on the other side of the gym. She knew he was watching but remained indifferent. Jonathan fumed quietly and at the end of the two hours, raced off to the shower in a huff. Ginn chuckled quietly as she approached the woman's area to do the same.

Ginn took her time in the shower. Yet another move that infuriated the impatient and selfish Jonathan. The man hated waiting for anything and usually let it be known no matter if it was a restaurant, gas station or grocery store line. The only reason he accepted the current torture was the curiosity for the young woman. Thirty minutes later, fully dressed and made up, Ginn appeared and Jonathan thought to himself, the wait paid off.

"Shall we have a late lunch?" He smiled and once again opened the door for the lady.

"Sure." Ginn smiled and suggested a little eatery in town.

Jonathan had never heard of the place but played along. He wanted to make sure he bagged the prize.

The woman followed him to his car. "You don't have a car of your own?"

"Actually, no I was here with my friends and they left. So, I am all yours."

"That works for me." Jonathan beamed and sped through town while making small talk here and there. But Ginn rattled off question after question. She wanted to know everything about him. Jonathan didn't mind. His favorite subject was his success and what it took to get there. He figured she would be like the rest trying to be extremely interested but by day three he would oust her like the rest.

"I've never eaten at this place, looks a little beneath my dietary needs." Jonathan judged the mom and pop establishment before giving it a try.

"Are you ever grateful for anything?" Ginn's question sidelined the man. Needless to say, he took offense.

"I am grateful for many things. Which is why I work hard to keep my appearance, my job and my lifestyle where they should be. I have been able to do so by avoiding places like this."

Ginn returned a sarcastic, raised brow. They entered the place and found it to be clean and spacious. Ginn spoke to a few people then the pair sat down to eat.

Jonathan questioned the woman about her choices and replied with negative comments every time. Before long, he realized the cruelty of his words and toned things down. There would be "happy ending" if he kept on hounding her.

"I understand your opinions, Jonathan." Ginn took a sip of the sweet tea. "And you are entitled to them. Just always remember. Words can write checks that our Karma can cash in very devious ways."

Jonathan shrugged and nodded and kept the conversations to a minimal and only on discussed the basics. Nothing in depth surfaced to keep tempers at a lull and opinions to oneself. Afterward, as the day quieted into a muggy, hot evening, the couple ended up back at Fountain's massive abode. It was impressive for a single man with no family or significant other. Everything in the place mirrored the tastes of the owner. Trophies from past accomplishments lined the wall in frames and stood in cases at various points of the home. Pictures of vacations abroad, beach homes and selfies abounded.

"Is there anything that you love more than you, Mr. Fountain?" Ginn's tone reeked of sarcasm.

"I told you. I have worked hard to get where I am. Is it not impressive?"

"Oh, I am impressed. But not with your display. Now kiss me."

The couple embraced in a passionate kiss that led to even more passionate love making in the large, California king bed. Between Vera Wang sheets, the couple made love over and over until way into the wee hours of the morning. After a quick shower and change of sheets, they slept. When they awakened, it would be afternoon. This time, Jonathan chose the eatery and ordered from one of the more expensive places in town. He prepared the table, while she slept. Something in him wanted to win Ginn over to his side of things. He truly felt that the "top shelf" life was way more accommodating that just getting by.

"Time for a real meal." He whispered in her ear to waken the sleeping beauty then gave her one of his t-shirts and pajama bottoms. In a slow motion, Ginn strolled down the hall to the feast.

"I decided to skip my diet for the day and order something more robust. I hope you like it." The attorney pulled out her seat and served the meal.

Scrumptious potatoes, steak and lobster not to mention the salad, garlic rolls, and dessert were all displayed in a manner that graced the eyes in favor.

"This is very nice, and I appreciate the gesture."

Those were the only words that escaped her lips. The exchange left Jonathan bewildered. In the past, the displays of his wealth and prowess always garnered him a giddy "wow" or an oversized schoolgirl smile. But this time something made the man uneasy and filled him with fear.

After the meal and another round of love making, which ended in his hot tub, the couple sipped wine and talked. Jonathan, clearly irritated, began snapping at his date. Ginn responded with a calm that unnerved him even more.

"I see that my company is no longer welcomed."

"I don't understand you. You're not like..." The man stopped himself.

"The others." Ginn completed the sentence. "I'm not like the others. The ones who swooned over your power in bed and swayed at your extensive credit card use. Those things don't impress me."

"Then what the fuck does?" Jonathon's tone grew dark. He didn't like being prey.

"I'll make it easy for you. What is your wish now, Jonathan?" Ginn's disposition invited his vile comments.

"I wish you would get the fuck out. I never want to see you again. You will never be good enough for me."

"Well done, Jonathan. But I will leave you with one word. Hunger." And with that, the woman stood, got dressed and left. Jonathan felt defeated as he cursed and cleaned the table where they had feasted. Later on that night, the moment replayed in his head. Something felt wrong.

The following morning, Jonathan awoke with a strange sensation. After his normal routine, the feeling grew stronger. He had to eat. The man ran to the kitchen and began to devour everything in his path whether cooked or not. Raw eggs, spinach, carrots, juices, lunch meats, an even the leftovers from the night before, nothing satisfied the hunger. Before long, the phone range. It was his office. It was 11 o'clock and no one had heard from him.

"I'm sorry. I'm coming down with something and I've been in the bathroom all morning. I won't be in today."

His boss, a kind and caring individual, asked if he could do anything for him. Jonathan's replied gracefully and ended the call.

For a moment, the hunger quieted, and he fell into a deep sleep. But when he awoke things were much worse.

The feel of the wind and the sound of water eased the man to awaken. His senses filled with the smell of earth and something primal. Jonathan was no longer home. He sat up and looked around. The big city lay in view almost as if he could touch it. The black waters of the St. Johns lapped just below his feet. *What the hell.*

Jonathan soon realized there were other developments. His clothing had been ripped as if in a struggle and he was covered in blood. The coppery taste and crusted aftermath aligned the man's lips which and made him retch and vomit. What came up was more horrific evidence of something foul.

The foul smelling, acid filled puke, chunked its way out. From the looks of it, the contents of the fridge reappeared along with something else. The thing was small, round and cloudy with nerve strings still attached. His hands shaking, he reached for it and prayed. A human eyeball lay amongst the remains of the rotted stench that had filled his gut. The man cried out loud as the other contents were not just from his fridge, but from a person.

Jonathan ran to the water to wash the filth from his body as best he could. With tattered clothing, he raced through the wooded area like an animal escaping a captor all the while searching for a way home. The hunger began to call once again. Tears flowed down the man's face and he dropped to his knees. With heightened senses, the animals in the dense woods scurried about. They knew something wicked now inhabited the land. The overall feeling of starvation took hold and all he could do now was dig. The hands that once typed pages and pages of depositions, letters and correspondence now dug deep into the earth for food. Nothing was safe and nothing seemed to help. He piled handful upon handful of dirt, grubs, crickets and whatever he could find into his mouth.

Back on his feet, the man ran as fast as he could until a familiar sight lay up ahead. The streets began to look more familiar. Jonathan recognized the surroundings. The river was only a mile or two away from the subdivision. He was home, but even that brought turmoil.

After punching in the key code to the back door, he gained entry. The house lay still, dark and dismal. It felt like home, but it didn't. Jonathan ran to the shower stripping off what remained of his clothing. The hot water and fresh soap made everything better, but the sense to hurl overwhelmed him. Dirt, worms, grubs, bugs and everything else from the woods now splattered about the marble tile and glass door. Jonathan began and cry and scream aloud, "WHY?!" He sunk down in the corner just beneath the soft water flow and sobbed. Once out of the shower, he searched for his cell phone. It was dead, which made no sense. He hadn't been gone that long or so he thought.

He secured a charger from the kitchen and brought the device to life. A range of shocked events unfolded as alerts and warnings flashed across the screen. Some wild animal was on the loose and had killed some boaters at a nearby dock. So far three bodies had been found. The murders took place at the river about 10 miles from where he slept. There were no other details, but one thing stood out. It had been three days since he saw his home or contacted the office. Several notifications displayed on the screen most were from the job. Worried about the absent employee, the office tried to reach him. They also did a well check, but there was no answer.

Jonathan sat alone in baggy clothes that no longer fit due to his new "diet." With ashy skin and sunken eyes, his appearance resembled nothing of the man he usually saw when he looked in the mirror. A pounding headache and churn of the stomach alerted him to another round of hunger. He cried out in the dark for it to stop.

The refrigerator remained bare from the last raid. He had to think fast before the fog settled in. He ordered several large pizzas for delivery. It seemed like forever and he cursed the time as it crept by. When the driver arrived, Jonathan shoved tip money into his hands and pushed him away. He knew what he was capable of and didn't want to hurt another soul nor have any contact.

Once again at the beautiful table where he had feasted with the mysterious Ginn, he now woofed down slice after slice of meat topping pizzas. He tore through the first three with ease and ordered six more. The same delivery guy appeared, and the same routine occurred. Jonathan shoved the money into the man's hand, grabbed the boxes and this time, plopped right in the floor and began to devour the pies. The driver backed away in fear. He knew something was wrong. Back at the store, he requested to not go back out to the man's house if he called again.

With six more pizzas in his gut, a calm took over. With more rational thoughts, his memories began to return and all the horrendous things he did surfaced. Before passing out, a familiar face, a casual smirk played in his mind.

"Ginn."

He said her name in quiet over and over. The memories of the scene at the river began to unfold. What was once foggy was now clear.

In one of the hunger induced spells, he wandered to the river. He had been on his feet for a while, but the smell of their flesh, so sweet and tender danced on the muddy river air. He stalked them in the quiet, thick of the nearby woods and took them out one by one. They had no idea what was happening. He tore out their throats disabling their ability to call for help. With blood spurting into the evening air, it appeared as if a macabre paint job had been performed on the nearby trees and shrubs.

Their flesh was salty, sweet and ripped from the bones with little effort. He was much more powerful in this state of starvation and overcoming his prey was too easy. Their tears and struggled intoxicated him more causing a blood induced fury. He finished them all within an hour.

As he dozed off yet again, tears flowed down his cheeks and one last memory played out. The wish. Ginn. *I've got to find that bitch and make her pas.* Jonathan drifted off into a deep sleep hoping the nightmare would end soon. When he awoke, the sound of thunder and boomed just above his head. He was outdoors again, but this time, the prey was very different.

A wicked storm rolled in overnight and dumped layer after layer of heavy rain. The only problem was that he was no longer in the floor of his kitchen. Once again, he found himself in a strange place and covered in blood. But he had a visitor.

"So, I see your sins have caught up with you, my dear Jonathan."

Ginn stood in the deluge laughing at the damned man.

"You did this!" Jonathan tried to pounce at her but could not move far. He looked down to see his ankles chained to a large pole.

"What the hell are you? What is happening to me?!"

Ginn chuckled at the once fit, athletic joke.

"You see, I grant wishes you idiot. And you were the easiest target."

"I didn't wish for..." He remembered his last words before she left. He screamed. "That's not fair."

"You didn't treat life fairly so why should I care about you? People like you pissing on the less fortunate so you can be a winner. I watched you for weeks at that gym. But you had nothing nice to say about me until I looked more like you."

Ginn waved her hand and gone was the slender blonde. Her true self now revealed, she was a short, thick woman with long dark hair that she kept in a braid, dark brown skin the color of coffee, rich dark eyes and a mole to the right side of her lip. He remembered her now and his remarks. "People like that need to work out at home. We don't need to see that."

"I'm sorry. I'll change. I promise I will change." Jonathan wept heavily. "Please remove the curse."

"Oh. Too late for that. Much, much too late."

Jonathan hurled once again and fragments of another murdered human emerged. The blackouts were very unpredictable, and now he understood there was no control. Weak, frail, and beaten he lay in the mud face down.

"Just get it over with."

Ginn smiled as she held out her blade.

"With pleasure."

# Lachelle Redd

Lachelle Redd is an indie author located in north central Florida. She has a number of titles in the horror, and fantasy genre and all are located on Amazon. She is currently working on a new release in her Hot Cauldron anthology and hopes to have it out by the end of the month. In her spare time, she enjoys movies and meeting other authors at comic cons in her local area.

# It Came: 2020
# Brandon Swarrow

He uses his left thumb and forefinger to gently pry apart thin horizontal window blinds. The worn white plastic offers zero resistance.

"Oh yeah, there she is," he murmurs while peeping obsessively.

A copper colored, slightly rusted, Dodge minivan slows to a stop near a neighboring mailbox. The sun rests just above a westward row of neighborhood rooftops. The vile minivan recoils and the lone functioning brake light shuts off.

The man behind the cheap window blind whispers, "Oh yeah, there's my girl."

The driver's window slides down.

"Yes, here it comes." The man adjusts his prying fingers to widen the blinds a little further. After affirming his grip, a lengthier, "Herrrre iiiiit commmes," passes through throat and lips.

A dense blotchy white and purple arm, waffles from the Dodge's upholstery. The hand is extending slowly toward the mailbox.

Whispering only exclusively through exhalation, the man, "Oh shit, oh shit, look at that thick-ass arm flab."

The man begins panting in rhythm, "You got it girl, go for it, Jerk it, yank it, come on, pull it."

The flabby arm withdraws. Can't reach. The upper torso of a plump middle-aged female now defies gravity by hanging halfway out of the van's window. A heavy hand pulls downward on the mailbox's door.

From behind rapidly shaking window blinds, a foghorn-like lengthy groan is heard.

The woman in the Dodge van pulls one large singular brown envelope from the box.

The man behind the blinds is making savage grunt-like sounds in short whispering bursts, which build up to a barely audible squeak.

So red, so bold, like an analog alarm clock on a moonless night, the words EVICTION NOTICE appear in all caps. She reels in the letter, as well as her fat upper half, back into her vehicle. The van dips and rocks in reaction to the return of her rump to her seat. The disheveled Dodge dashes approximately twenty feet up the driveway and then halts inside of an unkempt garage. A garage door, gliding slowly downward, steals the view.

The peeping man removes his forefingers from the blinds, the plastic smacks together, but no dust specks fill the day air. His left hand drops to his pudgy side. He turns, the back of his shirt is wet and contours humped posture.

It takes immense exertion for the man to drag his slouching body over toward his living room sofa. With heavy sliding feet, the man turns around, now facing season 31 episode 666 of The Simpsons.

Backside first, the man plops down on the couch like it is his personal trust-fall. A coalescence of food crumbs and dust particles billows outward from his now limp body. The man inhales extensively, and then groans out a long spent "ahhhhhhh". He folds both hands behind his head, and rests one leg at a time upon a grimy coffee table. He whispers one word before gently closing his eyes... "Merica'"

# Brandon Swarrow

Brandon Swarrow has four fiction novels; The Barn, Hugo Read This!, The ThrillPlex Theater, and his most recent Coulro. He has also published several short stories, and poems. Brandon currently resides near Pittsburgh, PA with his wife Michelle and two children.

# An Alternate Path to Redemption
## Greg Bennett

"**G**ET OUTTA HERE, YA DAMN MUTT!"
Frank's leg kick swung wide as the tiny blur of tan streaked by, just out of reach of his foot. With a high-pitched yelp, it ran haphazardly across the living room, knocking over empty beer cans and pizza cartons, before bolting headlong down the dark side hallway. Toenails losing grip on the slick linoleum flooring, it slid sideways into the wall as it bounded and disappeared into a back bedroom.

"STAY OUTTA MY CHAIR! THAT GOES FOR ALL YOU LITTLE SHITS!"

Standing among crumpled paper napkins scattered about the floor, Frank kicked away some of the beer cans and sat down in his recliner.

*They were just one more thing. One more ass-wipe thing to deal with.*

*It seemed everyone was on his case to get him to do something.*

*The last time he was there, the idiots at the doctor's office had nagged at him to exercise more, and watch his diet. They told him he needed to schedule regular checkups. They talked about heart disease, cholesterol shit, and some other potential diabetic problems. He didn't know much about that medical stuff and didn't really care. Shit, he felt fine.*

*Sure, he was overweight some, but he didn't think he was huge by any means. He'd seen other losers, much worse than him.*

*They even told him he was a "high risk" candidate for that Covid virus crap that was going around. That he needed to wear a mask any time he was out in public. Yeah, like that's gonna happen. Stupid quacks.*

*Then, there was his sister and her mangy, flea-bitten dogs.*

*His darling little sister, Suzie. She and her miserable excuse of a husband, Tom, were going on some vacation in the upper states, and then doing some remodeling work on their house. You'd think with all the money they had to blow on vacation and their home, they'd have enough to take care of their dogs. But, noooooo, she approached him and performed the greatest sob-and-guilt story he'd ever heard. It was "Oh, but we're family", and "But this is our livelihood", and "It would only be for two to three weeks and they'd be so grateful and...and..."*

*After he'd finally agreed to take care of them (she was family, after all), that's when she mentioned there were EIGHT of the little bastards. Eight purebred Chihuahuas they used for breeding services. Eight, ten-pound furry meat-bags with toenail-clicking feet. Shit.*

Frank turned and opened a beer from the small cooler he kept at the side of his chair.

His sister had given him instructions on how to care for the dogs, but they were way too complicated.

The dogs required a special diet, with special food, feeding times, and lots of water.

He didn't have a problem with the water; he found one of those continuous feeding jug things that held enough water for at least a couple of weeks.

The food, however, was a pain in the ass. One-third cup per dog, three times a day, first feeding with the high protein, second feeding with some special luminous coat food...he couldn't remember what the third feeding used. Special food, feeding times, it seemed that's all he did each day.

The kicker was, his sister didn't leave enough food. When she dropped them off, she left enough for a few days, and said she would return with more, but didn't. He tried to call her, but only got her voicemail.

He wasn't about to spend his hard-earned cash on some fancy, expensive food for the mutts. He found a bag of store-brand food that looked like it would work. He didn't worry about the feeding schedule; they got fed when he got around to it. Even when he managed to feed them, they always seemed hungry.

He didn't have much room in his rental home, it was too small to begin with.

His sister had set them up in the spare bedroom. She had unfolded and secured several small wire cages with foam pads. A couple of the dogs used each cage, and seemed to be content with each other's presence.

She told him that they should be fed elsewhere, to avoid making a mess. They decided an open area of the kitchen floor would work for that purpose.

The house had a fenced backyard, so he could at least let the dogs out to do their business. Trouble was, they could never do their business altogether. It seemed that at least one of them whined constantly about wanting out. Accidents happened routinely; he tried to clean up the worst of them.

Tired of cleaning up the wet messes, he placed a bunch of pee pads all over the bedroom floor. When the ammonia smell became unbearable, he disposed of the wet pads and replaced them.

He didn't know why he let her talk him into taking care of the dogs. It wasn't as if she had done him any great favors. He guessed that, deep down, he wasn't necessarily a bad person, just maybe a lazy one.

It was a lot to think about. It was already late in the afternoon, so he decided it was time to watch some boob tube and let his mind relax from all his worries and frustration.

THE BEER IN HIS LEFT hand was still somewhat cold. As he lifted the can to his mouth, he suddenly couldn't hold it as it tumbled from his hand and bounced on the floor, sloshing beer in a foamy, amber arc as it splashed on the chair and his pants. His hand, and then his entire arm, felt weird...felt...numb. Suddenly, he began to feel a dull pain radiating down his arm and stared as his arm began to twitch uncontrollably. He struggled to stand up, but a wave of dizziness overcame him, and he reeled forward as the pain of a thousand ice picks pierced his chest. Falling to the floor, he rolled onto his back with arms and legs splayed, unable to move, unable to cry out. His mind and body overwhelmed by paralyzing pain, he stared with open eyes as the room slowly faded to darkness.

The next morning, the dogs awakened, stretched, and scurried about the back room. Some were playfully nipping at each other; others just casually sniffing around the room. Fully awake, they gradually made their way to the back area of the kitchen, where they were normally fed.

There was no food.

They sniffed around the empty bowls and, finding nothing, worked their way into the living room. The pizza boxes smelled delicious, but all were empty.

Some of the dogs gave a "feed me" bark and sat at the front door, watching with expectant eyes.

Nobody came.

And they were hungry.

Later in the afternoon, the dogs were getting restless. No one had come through the front door. No one had called for them with food to feed them. They ran from room to room, but nobody was there. There was no food.

And they were hungry.

A couple of the dogs barked at the prone figure on the floor. The furless alpha didn't move.

While the others explored the living room, one of the larger male dogs known as "Augie" cautiously approached the alpha's face.

Augie stretched and sniffed the alpha's face, nose and mouth. The smell of pizza and beer was strong, and Augie could still smell the alpha's normal distinctive smells, but something was...different.

Glazed, the alpha's eyes were still open. Unblinking.

His open mouth and visible teeth made him appear as if he was trying to say something, but there was no sound, no movement.

Augie cocked his head and stared at him. Unconsciously, Augie licked his lips.

Moving in almost slow motion, a petite female named "Bitsy" approached and sniffed one of the alpha's hands. Still covered in pizza grease and beer; the smell and taste were intoxicating. A cautious lick at first, and then licking furiously, she lost control...and bit one of the fingers.

There was no reaction from the alpha. No snarl, no movement.

The pizza grease and blood gave the flesh a succulent flavor. She bit harder, scraping bone with her tiny, pointed teeth.

Still, no movement.

As a domesticated pet, she had been taught to fear and obey the furless alphas. Now, however, her hunger and survival instinct drove her to a new transition; one that typically happens quickly and easily in the wild animal world. The furless alpha was no longer her master. He was...food.

Emboldened, she began to feed, teeth grinding bone and flesh as she found herself in canine ecstasy.

The scrawny female named "Aster" soon joined her and quickly began to gnaw on a couple of the other fingers; the sounds of crunching bone attracting the attention of the other dogs.

Drawn by the crunching sounds, a stocky male named "Frankie" joined Augie at the alpha's face. Driven by hunger, Frankie licked, then gnawed at a corner of the alpha's mouth. The soft, pink flesh tore away easily, leaving a gaping, ragged hole in the alpha's jaw, exposing jaw muscles and rows of teeth.

Together, they tore the flesh away from the face, yanking the cartilage from the nose and ears. Feeding with total abandon, they soon reduced the alpha's face to a skeletonized mask of crimson, with eye sockets staring into oblivion.

Attracted by the sound from the other dogs, a small female named "Peanut" approached the alpha's neck and ear. Sniffing, she, too, found herself drawn to the succulent pizza smells that seemed to be everywhere. She licked the soft flesh along the neck and soon found herself scraping her teeth along the upper part of the shoulder. Resistance gone, she sank her teeth into the clavicle, tearing the thin layer of flesh away. Biting and chewing the juicy flesh, she had soon removed most of it, leaving the bloody bone exposed.

The rest of the dogs soon joined in, ripping and tearing flesh as they feasted upon the large, still figure on the floor. Exposed skin from clothing, nose, ears, throat, all ripped away as the dogs fed in a blood-soaked frenzy.

Two of the dogs were chewing on the clavicle bones and, with herculean effort, tore them from the chest. This provided a larger opening into the top of the chest, exposing other soft tissues. Soon, other dogs were burying their heads inward, and pulling out the soft flesh they could reach; the rest of the throat, the trachea, the top of the lungs.

Some of the dogs ate until they could no longer eat; left to throw up; then returned for more.

Their tiny bodies covered in blood, they were vicious, fearless, and uninhibited.

Maybe it was revenge for being mistreated, or perhaps it was a reversion to wild instincts. It didn't matter.

The flesh was plentiful. The flesh was delicious.

And what about Frank, who had made himself the epitome of laziness and self-loathing? Well, he finally came through; providing a bountiful and immensely satisfying meal...on time.

# Greg Bennett

G reg Bennett is a Regulatory Compliance manager who lives with his wife in western Missouri, USA. When he isn't slaving away at his engineering day job, he enjoys playing golf, cycling and being an aspiring writer; influenced by his longtime love of 'B-movie' science fiction and horror.

He brings an 'Average Joe' style to his writing; one that places ordinary people in extraordinary situations.

Focusing on drabble, flash and short-story work; several of his efforts have been published in various well-received anthologies, some of which have been for notable charitable causes such as the Wounded Warrior Project.

# Hell, at the Tele-Art
# Danny Campbell

Yes, the sign reads badly, awkwardly, I know. But I spent seven hundred pounds on it. SEVEN hundred! And besides, what do these people care anyway? They just want to spend their money on things that remind them of their childhoods. Personally speaking, childhood was an oppression that I longed to be free of. Yes, I hated my parents and wished them dead frequently. No such luck, though, they are still living and seem to be enjoying life whereas I never have.

Welcome to my shop. Do you like it? Yes, there are lots here for you if like trinkets, plastic dolls, board games, game and movie themed retro, vintage stuff of the kind popular thirty years ago, now you've made a bit of money, have a mortgage, and want to inflict your own, miserable childhood on brats of your own. Ideal for a hipster shit hole like Upper Street. Yes, it really fancies itself, does Upper Street. Even the name, Upper, right, like up your own arsehole. Think of the tele-art as a Forbidden Planet for those who cannot be bothered to drag their arses up to Shaftesbury avenue on a Saturday morning. Oh well, tired of London, tired of life and all that.

How did I get here? Like the Talking Heads song, I suppose, but it's really down to Senor Zapatero. I mean, I had to sell my own arse, and if you're going to do something like that, you'd better get paid well. At least that's the way I see it. No hanging around Soho clubs or Hampstead Heath for long nights and a sore arse for shekels and a crack habit. No, fuck that, I wanted money in the bank. I mean, what else is there? I am, there is no doubt, a greedy, lazy, and, I would not argue against it, a resentful man.

You see, I'm really a very unlikeable person, but many single-minded people are. You know, when they do that share ten albums that influenced you, and ten films that changed your life, all that self-congratulatory bollocks on Facebook, no-one ever thinks to ask me!

But it doesn't matter, because I'm rich, and the rich always have the last laugh, don't they? Look at them piling in; bearded man-boys in tight pink trousers, their wives and girlfriends placating nappy filling despots in the making, and all the while, the contactless payments keep piling up. So much better than working for a living. All I do is search, buy, and sell. I've even started playing the stock market a little.

If I have anyone to thank for my present state, it is the rich Spaniard I have already mentioned. I know that I paid my dues in arse flesh, but he rewarded me kindly, set me up like this, not many people in this world have either the means, or the inclination to do that. But, you know, a slave, even a well kept one, is still a slave, and my benefactor occasionally lets me know. Just a little interference, for sure, a comment here, a little refusal for credit there, so I know for sure who is really in control. But tell me, did you ever hear of a slave falling in love with his master? I don't mean in some long winded, orgasmic fantasy of the landed gentry's flirtation with literature, falling in love with gardeners and chimney sweeps and all that Victorian bollocks, I mean really, who loves the legs, hips, back, and fatuous head of the one who has a foot in your back?

It can take a lot to control one's tongue, but I was in it for the long run. You noticed that I said was, did you? How very astute. Yes, it was the long run, or the long game, in it till the end, till death do us part, etc and ad infinitum. Look it was a few years, right. Long enough that when the moment came to extricate myself, or perhaps extricate Senor Zapatero is more correct, from the picture, I was more than ready for it. Don't you just love that word 'correct'? I do. It means so many things right in a world gone so wrong. My personal, all time favorite is when Delbert Grady, after washing advocaat off of Jack Torrance's fashionable, 1980s suede jacket says, "I corrected them, sir, and, when my wife tried to prevent me from doing my duty, I, corrected her." It's always stuck in my mind as the best way to deal with a problem. But then again, that's me. Anyhow, I corrected my life much in the same way Mr. Grady corrected his.

It was and it wasn't planned. I mean, I had planned to do it, but maybe not at that precise moment. I just could not look at that flaccid winky anymore, with senor spunky expecting me to breathe some life back into it. No. There comes a time for everything, including, if you are so built as I am, for murder.

He just stood there with that stupid, entitled look on his face, the way he had always looked at everything. Easy when you are born into a rich, liberal family in Madrid, with a little aristocratic blood flowing through your veins, and as much money as you can eat enshrined in a trust for perpetuity. Too easy, you can have almost anything you want, and if not exactly love, then as good an approximation of it as you'll ever need. Look at Donald Trump.

Anyway, I was saying, yes, he stood there in his underpants, his long, white ponytail hanging over his shoulder, tied up with a velvet ribbon (he'd never got past the 1980's fashion wise), with that have-your-cake-and-eat-it smile, that perennially irritating, vulturine eye. I smiled back, and I don't think he noticed, not until my hands began to tighten round his throat.

Then he noticed, all right, that vulturine eye nearly popping out of its socket. That Velvet tie suddenly falling away with what life remained in the old buzzard!

How he gurgled! I was almost ashamed. But the prize glistened before me. With him out of the way, there was only me, and that was all that ever mattered. I had the shop, the stock, the three-bedroom flat above it, the business and personal bank accounts.

Then there remained little Cervantes. Reader, this, I must confess, for you must imagine by now that I have never had a heart, is the most disagreeable aspect of this story. The dog had been watching, of course, terrified, and now I knew that there was nothing else I could do other than send it on its way with its beloved master. Everyone who we knew in the four years we had lived as a couple knew that Senor Zapatero and Cervantes would never be separated in this life. If one were to disappear, then so must the other.

He cowered in the corner as I approached him, he even growled, the little mite. But that cocksure, prissy, strutting attitude of the toy dog, imperious in the presence and protection of its owner, had vanished, and it was easy to scoop him up into my arms. He whimpered as I throttled him, and I could feel his heart racing beneath the fur. Boom-boom, boom-boom, boom-boom, then nothing; he fell limp in my arms. I suppose that is the moment I began to question myself.

I CLOSED THE SHOP FOR a few days for 'improvements', went to a DIY shop and bought some of that easy to put together, click-clack parquet. The digging was hard; I had to break up concrete to get to the earth below the back- kitchen of the shop, which needed a revamp. I am unaccustomed to manual labor, I can barely be bothered to go to the posh gym I'm a member of, unless it's for a sauna in the winter, so swinging a pick axe, after dragging the now defunct Senor Zapatero down the stairs, proved a little getting used to.

Sweat! I have never known the stuff to pour out of me like that! I was soon covered in a wet, sticky film of it, and had to change my shirt three times. By the time I stopped, and I stood there bare chested and panting, looking like I had pissed my trousers, the shirts in a heap on the floor smelled of urine. All the while, Senor Zapatero lying on the floor had stiffened up and his hands were clenched in a disabled grip, his face with a horrified, sad, and surprised expression, at least, I have to say, his eyes were closed.

Cervantes's, however, were open and glassy, and it is if he looked at me and said: whimper, boom-boom, boom-boom. I threw one of the piss smelling T shirts over him.

Six feet under, so they say, but I'd guess it was more like four. Wrapped up in plastic and concreted over, no-one was ever going to tell the difference anyway. Putting the parquet together was as easy as a jigsaw, but when that last piece went clack it was all over. There were soon a multitude of suede and leather trainers shuffling over the very spot where they lay, and, I'll tell you, when they lingered over it for too long, to look at something, or worse, to bend down and tie a shoe, it was more than a little distracting.

It was at night, however, after they had all gone, that the sounds started. Right on the dot, at six o'clock, after the last cheerful bastard had left my shop, whimper, boom-boom, boom-boom.

Then came the coppers' first visit. An anodyne pair, really, all excess flesh and ill fitted uniforms.

'We're inquiring about a report that a (pulls out notebook, looks at it) Mr., err, Senior, err, Zapatera, is it? Has disappeared without trace and a concerned relative in Spain would like us to ascertain his where-abouts,' the first one said in that dumb, rehearsed copper's voice he'd copied off the TV, while the other stared blankly at the shop's art objects, only raising an eyebrow when catching the price tag on them. They didn't present too much of a challenge. I simply told them that he had run away with a young dago he met while visiting his home country, that he was a wealthy man with homes in other countries of the world, and if he didn't want to be found he would be difficult to find. They chuckled at the word dago, and that is why I threw it their way, but after their little, conspiratorial snigger, they remembered that they were dealing with poof business, and wrinkled their noses accordingly.

Then the quiet one looked at me and said,

'You're sweating, sir, a bit hot?' Whimper, boom-boom, boom-boom, whimper, boom-boom, boom-boom.

'I...I...was, was moving some stock.'

'Very well sir, we'll take up no more of your time, but sir, please contact us if you have any new information on his whereabouts, will you?'

Yes, of course, of course I will.' Whimper, boom-boom, boom-boom.

IT DOESN'T STOP AND it's getting worse. Now I see the dog's face, a white, west highland terrier, a male with a pink ribbon holding up its fringe. Little Cervantes. I hardly think of Senor Zapatero at all, but that dog. It's affecting my sleep, my work. I need a generous amount of unctuous charm, not hollow-eyed irritability. I almost told a customer to fuck of, and that kind of thing would be a death knell for the types round here. There are always plenty of other bijou shops for them to waste their money in before pissing off over the road to eat at Ottolenghi's.

No, that won't do at all. But it isn't how I thought it would be, and the dead are proving more troublesome dead than when they were alive. At least then he would take off for weeks on end. Now he is permanently here. I got a rather nasty phone call from his sister Sanchia, accusing me of all kinds of things. I felt like I had had a real kicking afterwards I can tell you. It was "I know you did something! I never trusted you!", nice to know how you really felt, but I suppose she's not wrong. You ever get the feeling you have bitten off more than you can chew? What seemed such a good idea not long ago doesn't seem so now.

The coppers came back, different ones, ones who were much more icily forensic.

'Your shop was closed for a few days from 17th May till the 21st, could you happen to tell us the reason for that. Only Senor Zapatero's car has been found in a long stay car park at Gatwick airport, and his bank reports that someone has been accessing his money in the Islington area.'

'How the hell would I know? Look, he's left me in the lurch you know, I have to run this place on my own now and there are overheads.'

'What were you doing on those four days your shop was shut? Only the ticket for the long stay car park was bought on the 20th.'

'I...I...I.' No, not now. Shut up you stupid dog.

'Are you alright, sir?'

'What?'

'Your lips were moving.'

'No, it's just that...'

'Just what, sir? Is there something you would like to tell us about?'

'Just that I'm tired. Tired, damn it. Look I'm TIRED!'

'Calm down sir. It's only that we've had information from a Spanish woman, the missing person's sister. Here (pulls out notebook), a Ms Sanchia Zapatero. It appears that she's not very keen on you. She had a number of very unfriendly things to say about you, sir. Would you care to respond to them?'

'Look, that fucking woman hates me, always has, I, as it happens, could have a number of unfriendly things to say about her.' No, be quiet dog, fuck you Cervantes! Whimper, boom-boom, boom-boom.

'Are you sure you're alright? Mind if we look around?'

'What? Oh, OK, yes, I suppose...' So, it's always like this. One moment, we are in command, have engineered our lives, our plans, have fixed them to the wall of our imagination, determination. Then something petty comes along, or at least something less grandiose, something banal. Or what would be petty if it didn't consume us. Consume us with, with...yes, a sin, or several deadly sins. Greed, laziness, resentment. Greed, hatred, and delusion. What's the difference? It all adds up to the same thing.

'This a new parquet floor, sir? Very shiny.'

'What? Yes...' All blown over a dog's whimper. A dog! That slavish animal I never really could stand, yet at the same time, could never really hate. Now it's whimpering comes back to haunt me. The little furry, struggling ball now there under the cold ground.

The coppers are all over the place, their eyes, scouring, taking everything to pieces, taking me to pieces. There must be a way out of this hell, at the tele-art. Should I just run, take what money I can lay my hands on and go? That one, the one who thinks he's Columbo, he even has a lazy eye, not unlike Senor Zapatero's, he's into my skin now, scraping it from the inside, pulling away the fat and muscle, rattling my bones.

That spot on the floor, he's standing on it. Don't! Walk away, go upstairs, anywhere. Here come Cervantes's ghost crawling up through the new, wooden floor. Covered in mud, worms in his eyes. Now Senor Zapatero, gone is the vulturine eye, it too is a socket full of worms. He's stroking Cervantes's little body with a stiff, dead hand. Fuck off, will you?

Whimper, boom-boom, boom-boom.

The detective's cell phone rings, and the ring tone is Carmina Burana. Too much! Too much!

'Just get off there will you?' I shove the shabby bastard out of the way. 'I did it! Alright! Are you fucking happy now? They're there, under your feet, him and the little fucking dog. I don't care, just shut it up, shut it up.'

'I'm arresting you on the suspicion of murder of a Senor Zapatero, you do not have to say anything. But it may harm your defense if you do not mention when questioned something which you later rely on in court.'

'No more! No more! No more tell-tale heart!'

# Danny Campbell

D anny Campbell is the author of numerous novellas, essays and articles about Thailand and South East Asia, many of which are held in university libraries worldwide. Since moving to France in 2006, Danny has concentrated on work which reveals the hidden corners of his home city, Bordeaux, and its multifaceted cultural influences. He is working at present on a forthcoming novel entitled Lala's Nonstop Erotic Caberet.

# Seeing Green
# Sheri Velarde

Charley batted her eyelashes and laughed at the silly joke Henry just told. After another hair flip and a sultry lick of the lips, she decided it was time to make her move. With a glare she sent their other co-worker Sam scurrying for the bar to refresh his drink. Not missing her chance, Charley moved closer and put her hand on Henry's forearm. "You certainly have a lot of stories. Are all British men as exciting or charming as you?" She made sure to lean ever so closer to him, making sure he had a good view of her ample cleavage.

Henry gently pulled his arm back from her. "Well my girlfriend would tell you that I'm not half as charming or funny as I seem to think that I am."

"Girlfriend? I didn't know that you were seeing anyone." Charley said, fighting to keep the green eyed monster from slipping into her voice. "I thought you just moved here."

"Well Camille is still back in London at the moment, so we are doing the long distance thing for right now. I'm doing my best to convince her to come here to New York though. If she can get work lined up I think she will." Henry said with a wistful smile playing upon his lips.

Charley felt anger fuel her just from thinking of this unknown woman with the man she had deemed to be worthy of her time. No, a girlfriend would just not do. She would have to find a way to dispose of this Camille woman and the sooner the better. Soon Henry would be looking at her with that loving look in his eyes. She smiled at him, but he shot her a strange look.

"Are you feeling alright Charley? For a moment I thought I saw something wrong with your eyes... It must have just been a reflection or something; people's eyes don't change colors suddenly right?" He let out a nervous laugh. "Let's go join the others at the bar; I think I could use some food before I have another drink."

Slightly put off by his wanting to be with their other coworkers, Charley tried to squelch the resentment building inside of her. Henry was new to their firm and just getting used to living on this side of the pond. It's only natural that he clung to some things back home, like his soon to be ex-girlfriend. She had always gotten the men she wanted and she had never wanted anyone as bad as she wanted Henry. He would be hers, but she would let him take it slow if that's what he needed. Soon he would forget all about London and this Camille chick.

ANOTHER WEEK WENT BY and Charley found herself out once again with Henry, well Henry and their fellow coworkers. She still hadn't managed to get much alone time with the elusive Brit yet, but tonight she planned to pull out all the stops. She had brought a change of clothes specifically for this evening, an outfit that she knew Henry would not be able to take his eyes off of. When she walked into the bar a little after everyone else had gotten there, he and everyone else's eyes had about popped out of their sockets. Yes, tonight would be her night to finally land Henry once and for all.

Everything was going to plan. Charley made sure she sat next to Henry, looking gorgeous of course. She laughed and flirted and kept his drink full at all times. Tonight he would not be able to resist her. As time went on, the more intoxicated they all became and Henry leaned to her and whispered, "You are a beautiful woman Charley. If I didn't have a girlfriend..."

She smiled, knowing that she had just won. "Well you don't have a girlfriend; you know long distance relationships never work."

Henry stared at her, his eyes a bit dazed from drink and lust for her. He started to move in as if to kiss her when they both heard his name called from somewhere behind him. "Henry!"

Henry immediately snapped out of his daze and turned towards the female voice calling him. Charley reached for his arm, trying to turn his attention back towards her and what had been about to happen, but to no avail. He not so gently pulled out of her grasp and all but ran to meet the tall, leggy blonde who had caused this disruption. "Camille," he shouted as be grabbed her and pulled her into a passionate kiss. "I can't believe you are really here. Pinch me to make sure I'm not dreaming!"

Camille laughed and just kissed him again. "I'm really here and plan on staying!"

Henry and his girlfriend kept talking, but Charley couldn't hear what they were saying over the pounding in her ears. She had been so close, he had been about to kiss her when this British strumpet had to show up and ruin everything. She could feel the anger coursing through her, feel the hate for this woman, and envy for what should be hers. No, she would not lose what she wanted to this too skinny tramp. She was twice the woman of this Camille; she knew she had to be better than her in every way, which meant she would indeed get her man in the end. She would just have to figure out how to get rid of the girlfriend once and for all.

Her blood still felt as if it were boiling as Henry walked around, showing off his girl toy to all their coworkers. The other men in the office seemed to think she was gorgeous or something. As if. They were working their way towards her and she had to fight hard to get her face to show some semblance of a smile when what she really wanted to do was slap the shit out of this bimbo. "And last but not least this is Charley; she's been so friendly and welcoming as I try to settle in here."

Camille reached out her hand and smiled with perfect teeth, "Oh it's so nice to meet you. Henry speaks fondly of you, said you keep inviting him out and making sure he gets to know his coworkers and gets a feel for the city. How sweet of you." She flashed her pearly whites again before making gaga eyes at Henry. "I hope you'll extend your friendliness towards me as well."

When hell freezes over, Charley thought to herself as another wave of heat struck her. "Of course." She managed to say, though she doubted she conveyed any warmth in her voice when all she felt was hatred.

"Are you feeling okay? I swear your eyes just turned green, which is ridiculous as I can see they are a dark brown. How strange." Camille said, bewildered.

"I think it's something to do with the lights here. I've seen it happen before. I'm sure there is no green eyed monster lurking in Charley." Henry laughed, pulling Camille in for another hot kiss.

Charley's hands flexed, she swore her nails were actually lengthening as jealousy once again flooded her mind and body. Finally she managed to get herself under control. She couldn't have any angry outbursts. When Henry and Camille broke up he had to think that she had nothing to do with it, that she was just the kind friend who would help him through everything. Then should would remind him how beautiful he found her, show him that there would be life after Camille and that Charley could be a big part of that life. No, she had to play to perfect and sweet woman still, but she couldn't watch them kissing and drooling over each other anymore. "I don't know if it's the lights or if it's too hot in here, but I'm not quite feeling myself. I think I better call it an early night and head home." She quickly excused herself before she let her anger get the better of her, no her plans called for much more subtle sabotage.

THE WHOLE WEEKEND CHARLEY felt anger and envy building inside of her. She should have spent the past two days in bed with Henry, ensnarling him even further, but no Miss I had to come all the way from London to ruin plans was sharing his bed instead. No matter, Charley always got what she wanted even if she had to lie and cheat to get it. Henry would be hers; she just had to make his girlfriend disappear.

On Monday she visited Henry's office first thing in the morning, looking her best of course. She was shocked to see that some of their other coworkers were already in there, laughing and shaking his hand. Henry had barely worked there a couple months, so she doubted he'd been promoted already, so why were people congratulating him?

"Charley! Get in here and hear the news! I got engaged over the weekend! Camille is moving here permanently and we are getting married! Can you believe it?" Henry said, a huge smile on his handsome face.

"What? No!" She said, this could not be. She needed more time to get rid of the bothersome Camille. How could they have gotten engaged over the weekend? That flush of anger and envy rushed through her body again, only strong than ever before.

She felt so hot, so confused. She took a step back and stumbled. Henry rushed forward and grabbed her before she could fall. At his touch she felt herself almost lose control; she wanted to take him right then and there. She wanted to make him hers now and forever. But she couldn't do that, not here in the office in front of all their coworkers. That would not be playing it cool. But why was she finding it so hard to control herself?

"Whoa there, are you okay Charley? I'm the one getting married here and should be feeling faint." Henry joked as he looked at her with concern. "Seriously are you okay? You don't look so good. Are you still feeling ill?"

Getting ahold of herself, she pulled Charley stumbled out of his grasp. Being close to him drove her crazy. "No, no I don't feel well at all. I think I need to go home. I'm sorry." She turned and rushed back towards the elevators. She needed to get out of here. As she looked down at her own hands her nails were turning black and growing, her skin turning a pale green before her eyes. What the hell was happening to her?

She heard Henry call after her, "Charley let me take you home. Or maybe to the doctor. I think you might be really sick."

Charley had basically broken into a run by then, reaching the elevator doors and beating the buttons to open the door. "No, I just need to get home. I'll be fine." She heard a crunching noise and looked down at the button she had been hitting, she had broken it somehow, but the elevator doors opened just then and she hurried in, also breaking the button to shut them. Where had this sudden strength come from?

Once she reached the ground floor she bolted out of the building, running faster than she ever had in her life. She actually heard people scream as she ran by, which only made her run faster. She could feel her toenails growing and digging into her shoes, her skin kept darkening into a putrid green color. This couldn't be real; she was just having a terrible dream brought on illness and envy. That had to be it. Any minute now she would wake up in her apartment, tired but still as beautiful as ever. She just needed to find a way to wake herself up. "Wake up!" She shouted at herself, but even her voice didn't sound like her anymore.

At last she saw her apartment building; she had run through half of Manhattan in just minutes, which should have been impossible. It didn't matter, she needed to get inside, to look in the mirror and see what was really happening to her. She didn't even bother with the elevator in this building; she just bolted up the stairs, taking them three at a time. In seconds it seemed she unlocked her apartment door. She was home. Now she could calm down and find a rational explanation for everything.

Safe in her own apartment, Charley kicked off her shoes and finally looked down at her own body. What she saw wasn't her at all; it was the body of a monster. Shaking her head and not accepting any of this, she went into her bedroom and looked in the mirror and screamed.

The only thing that remained the same was her long, black hair. The rest of her she couldn't even fathom. Here normally rich brown eyes were a murky green now with no pupil in sight. Her face looked distorted, some of her features were still there, but they were elongated and strange looking. Not to mention that her entire body seemed to be covered in a fine layer of puke green fur. Both her finger and toe nails were long and black, like the talons of a beast.

Freaked out, Charley slapped herself hard across the face. "Wake up!" She shouted once more. Nothing happened again, the horrifying sight before her remained. She had become some sort of demon, even though rationally she knew that could not be the case. People didn't just turn into devils from fairy tales, that's not how the real world operated. This had to be a dream, or rather some sort of nightmare that she couldn't wake from.

Yes, that had to be it. This was a nightmare brought on by that stupid Camille showing up and ruining Charley's plans with Henry. It was all Camille's fault for sending her brain into this dreadful spiral of anger and envy. At the thought of Camille, Charley's very blood began to boil again. That British wench caused all of this. She needed to be dealt with. Once she was gone Henry would be Charley's and hers alone and then everything would return to normal.

A red fury took over Charley's brain, Camille being the only thing she could think of. Camille had to be at the root of whatever was happening her, she knew it. Before her thoughts of revenge could go too far though, a knock came at her door. "Charley? Are you okay? It's Henry, I'm concerned about you. I think you should let me take you to the doctor. Can you let me in?" She heard the object of her lust call to her. Immediately she began to calm down, she looked at herself and swore she seemed closer to her normal self. This proved that all she needed was Henry.

Still, she had somehow become part monster and couldn't let him see her like this. "I can't come to the door right now. I'm not quite myself." She called out and her voice sounded almost natural, though slightly high pitched.

"Charley you looked really sick at the office. You were literally green. I think you need to go to the hospital." Actual concerned laced Henry's voice.

Looking in the mirror once more, Charley shook her head. She didn't think that the hospital would know what to do with her now. This was something out of a horror movie, not a common ailment that could be cured with a shot or something. No, she couldn't go out anywhere until she figured out how to reverse whatever was happening to her. "I'm fine. I think I just need a few days to rest." She walked to the door; she could almost feel Henry from the other side. "Thank you for coming to check on me though. It really means a lot to me that you care."

"Of course I care. You were the first friend I made at work when I moved here." Henry said and the sweetness in his voice made Charley feel calm and she swore her nails and skin started to return to normal. That is until Henry continued, "I want you and Camille to be friends too. She could use someone like you now that she is moving her to be with me. Maybe I can call her and she can come sit with you until you start to feel better?"

At the mention of Camille Charley felt the anger growing in her again. A green haze filled her vision and this time she could actually feel her body shifting and changing. The green spread, her whole body had become a grotesque mass of fur and sinewy muscle. Both her finger and toe nails were long, black claws now. She heard her clothes rip as she seemed to shoot up to a new height. Inside her mouth she her teeth elongated into giant fangs. "Camille. This is her fault." She growled, though what came out of her mouth hardly sounded human.

"Did you say something?" Henry called from the other side of the door. "I think maybe I should call 911."

Charley swore she could hear him pull his phone out of his pocket. No, she could not let him call someone. He was so close, she could even smell him now. He smelled of man; sweat, cologne and... sex. She could still smell that other woman on him. That sent her over the edge. All reason left her, she operated on instinct now. Instinct brought about by anger. Without hesitation she ripped the door open and grabbed Henry's phone, crushing it in an instant. Then she looked up and saw the terror in his face, right before he turned and ran, screaming as he went. The part of Charley still inside the beast hesitated, she wanted Henry to look at her with lust, love, or concern, anything except fear. The monster she had become drove him away, which was not acceptable.

Henry disappeared into the elevator while the human side of her still pondered what was happening. Part of her still wondered how this could have happened to her at all. How could she have turned into a horror that had sent Henry fleeing from the very sight of her? This wasn't what she wanted. She just wanted Henry. Henry should be hers. Her thoughts became hazy again, feral even and her base instincts drove all rational thought from her head.

She ran, now on all fours, towards the stairs. She had to catch her prey. Once she reached the ground level, the people in the lobby screamed and ran to hide from her. She didn't spare them a glance, they didn't matter, only Henry did. Reaching the outside she began sniffing for him, quickly picking up his scent and following it. She raced towards the direction she could smell Henry strongest, until the scent abruptly disappeared. She looked both ways, he must have gotten in a taxi. She roared in frustration.

Vaguely she could hear more people screaming and running from her, but she couldn't worry about them, she needed to find Henry. She reached back into her conscious mind, her human mind, looking for his address. She had never been to his apartment, but she had looked up his address at work. Luckily her monster brain seemed to be able to process that information still, for she took off running in the direction of her obsession.

She sped through the city, scattering people as she ran at superhuman speeds. Darting across the street she didn't pay attention, getting struck by a taxi. It knocked her down but didn't seem to hurt her, she got up shaking and started her pursuit once more, again not noticing the commotion she left in her wake. Henry was the only thing on her mind, finding him and making him hers' forever. Once she found him she would convince him that he was meant to be with her and no one else.

The wind blew just then and she caught his scent once more. He was near, just up ahead. She put on an extra boost of speed. She was almost there, almost to her love. She could grab him and runaway with him, make him love her too. Camille would be forgotten and she could have her happily ever after with Henry. There he stood, she could see him now. He was outside his apartment, talking on the phone. She tried to run even faster, getting hit by another car and not even stopping this time. She had almost reached him, he turned to look at her, panic in his eyes then something stung her shoulder.

She kept running, though more stings were attacking her body. Suddenly she realized they weren't stings but gunshots. Someone had shot her. She whirled around looking for who would dare shoot her and saw a wall of police officers behind her, all with their guns raised and firing right at her. She tried to call out, "No, what are you doing?" But only a demonic growl came out. The cops kept firing, more and more bullet holes wracked her body. She tried to move towards them, to get them to stop shooting, but her movements were becoming sluggish. Looking down at her body Charley, if she was even still Charley, saw nothing but blood pouring down herself. She could feel the life-force leaving her body, she was too injured to make it out of this even with her strange new powers.

She turned once again towards Henry. He stood across the street, his eyes fixed on her with a look of horror in them. Camille stood by his side, their arms locked around each other as she tried to stumble towards them. "Not her." Charley managed to croak as she fell to her knees. "Not her." She said one last time before she collapsed, the last of her energy leaving her. Henry pulling Camille closer was the last thing she saw before her eyes shut forever and the sight still made her see green.

# Sheri Velarde

S heri Velarde lives in New Mexico with her spouse and their dog. Being an avid reader since an early age, she has wanted to be a writer for as long as she can remember. She has been writing all her life, but only recently started to actually try to pursue her dream of writing for a living. She specializes in all things paranormal and that go bump in the night. Her heart truly lies in exploring unknown worlds or adding the supernatural to our world. If it goes bump in the night or has magical connotations, Sheri writes about it.

She is constantly putting out new material, so it is best to keep up with her on her website **www.authorsherivelarde.weebly.com**[1].

During the day she works in accounting and is a certified personal trainer, in her spare time Sheri is an artist, independent comic writer/ artist and freelance non-fiction writer. She can often be found with her nose in a book, or playing various games with her spouse and their friends. This includes D&D and Warhammer. Yep, Sheri is a nerd and proud of it.

Links:

Website/Blog: **http://authorsherivelarde.weebly.com/**

Facebook: **https://www.facebook.com/AuthorSheriVelarde/**

Twitter: **https://twitter.com/Sher_V**

---

1.    http://www.authorsherivelarde.weebly.com

# The Devil's Desire
# Jason White

THE CAR SPED ONTO THE dirt track leading into the wilderness of Hawkswood Forest. Rain hammered against the front windscreen and the sound of thunder could be heard in the distance. Jessica sung along to the song on the radio, clearly enjoying the weather in front of her. A muffled sound could be heard from the boot of the mini Countryman she was driving.

"Mmm, help me! Get me out of here for fucks sake! What's happening?"

Rick kicked away at the inside of the boot with all it was worth, hoping that someone other than his girlfriend Jessica would hear. This was the last time he would go anywhere with her. She had asked him to turn around whilst she undressed, telling him it was a surprise. The next thing he knew he had woken up inside the boot of her car.

Stopping at a clearing, Jessica turned the engine off. She laughed as she heard the thud of Rick's trainers against the boot. She felt it best to let him out before he suffocated . Opening the car door, she unbuckled her seatbelt and slid out. Her short skirt slid up, revealing long legs tanned to perfection. Going to the back of the car, she opened the boot. Rick squinted as she shone her mobile phone torch light straight into his eyes.

"Get out of the car! Move your arse before I kick the shit out of you! I'm not playing! Hurry up!"

Jessica grabbed Rick's black t-shirt in an effort to haul him up. He retaliated, making an attempt to grab her, but he fell back into the boot in his haste to chastise her for her so far successful kidnap attempt.

"Jess, what the hell have I done? Why have you brought me out to God knows where on Halloween night? I thought we were going round to your sister's to watch horror films? It is Halloween babe!"

Jessica stomped back and forth along the boot of the car, collecting her thoughts. This was a joke to her, but she had to make it look convincing. She rammed both fists on his chest, winding him, in an effort to look convincing that she was angry.

"Look you little fucktard! Get your arse out of the car! I haven't got time to play games. Unlike the games you have been playing with my sister! She told me you know!!"

Rick looked at her, puzzled. He hadn't touched Ronnie. She was gorgeous, but he was in love with Jess and she was a stunner. Long flowing red hair, petite figure, legs up to her armpits. Everything he had wished for and more. He clambered out of the boot, squelching his feet as they touched the forest floor. His designer trainers looked like a knock off from a broken into warehouse, but they had been ruined as soon as they had touched the sodden ground, soaked in mud and rainwater. He would remember not to buy suede again.

"Jess babe, let's talk about this please. I love you. You know I do. Your sister's a liar, I swear it beautiful."

He put out his hand to take hers. She proceeded to slap a handcuff onto his. Turning the phone light on again she shone it in the direction of some trees a few yards ahead.

"Walk over to the tree. Now!", she screamed. He thought it was best he played along, to keep her happy. As the rain increased in it's downpour of ferociousness he reached a tree which looked like a sweet bay magnolia.

"What do I do now?" he said.

Jessica raced in front of him, wrapping the loose handcuff around a tree branch and slapping it down onto his left wrist. He was now completely handcuffed. As much as he struggled he was unable to slide the cuffs over the tree branch and off. Rick could not see what Jessica was doing as she walked behind him, but he felt his t-shirt being cut, exposing his back and causing him to shiver as the cold rain hammered against it.

"You do nothing Rick, like the insignificant arsewipe you are. You don't shit on your own doorstep and that's what you did when you slept with my sister. You're scum! Now you're going to be punished!!!!"

Jessica left him and went to the car boot, reached inside and pulled out a leather whip. She cracked it as though she were auditioning for the lead role as Indian Jones.

"Now you're going to suffer!" she said, screeching like a possessed mad woman. She ran to him pulling down his jeans, revealing his muscly brown legs. His buttocks were firm, encased in black satin boxer shorts. His skin glistened with a thin veil of sweat, which left a subtle smoky condensation in the air. Hatred filled Jessica's brain, power over him intoxicating her senses. It was just a game, played by two very willing participants. She ran her hands over the satin boxer shorts, squeezing his buttocks until she heard an ecstatic moan emanate from his mouth.

"You like that, don't you? I think you preferred my sister's hands to mine though, seeing as you spent so much time at her house, doing D.I.Y. you shit!!!"

Jessica tore the satin boxer shorts off Rick with such force that he yelped as elastic snapped against his bare left buttock. She cracked the whip against his left buttock five times and he winced in pain feeling every stroke, clutching his buttocks together. He hoped it would dull the pain. The whip cracked against his right buttock for a further five times. This time he screamed as blood began to ooze from the lacerations she had etched into his skin.

"Jess, what the fuck babe! Stop! Please! I haven't done anything I promise. Please babe! I'm getting scared!!!"

Rick's voice was filled with anguish and despair. He had done nothing with Jess' sister. As much as he had been tempted. He remembered when he visited Ronnie's on one occasion and she had come into the living room, wearing her night dress. He had been painting the wall, when he felt a tap on his shoulder. Turning around he gasped as Ronnie let the night dress fall to the floor. His jaw had dropped as she stood there in black mesh basque, lace underwear and black stockings, held up by the sheerest of suspenders. He had looked at her and shook his head with a stern no. Turning around he had continued to paint the wall. She had then walked away in a huff, muttering under her breath. He thought that had been the end of it, but obviously not as Ronnie had spouted her poison to Jessica, clearly telling her a pack of lies, branding him an adulterer. How could he convince Jessica otherwise, he thought to himself.

"Confess Rick! Confess to your sins. Swear that you didn't touch an inch of her body. I'm waiting you piece of shit!!!"

Jessica pulled on the handcuffs, causing them to grip tighter against his wrists. He winced and could see she had no intention of relaxing her hold

"Jess babe! I've told you I never touched her! Ronnie's telling you lies babe! I love you with all my heart. There's no one else but you. Please!"

Rick started to cry, tears falling down his cheeks. Jessica relaxed her hold and went to the driver's side of the Mini Countryman and turned on the front headlights. His body was engulfed in the beam of light. The sight of his naked body made her squeal with excitement and she began to chuckle, clearly enjoying her escapade at his expense.

Going back to the driver's side door she leant in retrieving her mobile. Rick blinked as the flash on her phone shone into his eyes. She clicked away, taking numerous shots of him in the nude. She continued laughing and he looked in surprise as she produced the handcuff keys and made her way to unlock the handcuffs.

"Rick, you are such a glutton for punishment! You fell for my Halloween prank! You seriously thought I would believe you'd go for Ronnie over me? We also both agreed to come her and role play, but I thought I would make you think I'd lost my shit! Trick or Treat Rick!!!"

Jessica unlocked the cuff on his right hand and Rick gasped with relief. She then unlocked the cuff on his left hand, reaching in for a kiss. He responded by turning his face away to the left of him. She kissed him on the cheek.

"Your turn Rick. Handcuff me to the branch. I need to be punished my Lord. I have committed a crime and need to be dealt with, as only you can."

Jessica made her way over to the sweet bay magnolia and tugged at the black mini skirt she was wearing, until it dropped into a crumpled heap around her feet. She stepped out of the skirt, picked it up and placed it at the bottom of the tree trunk. Rick's heart started beating faster as he gazed at her long legs, which were encased in sheer black stockings. As his eyes travelled up her body, he moaned in anticipation as he gazed upon her beautiful pert buttocks encased in black lace panties. He wanted to rip the stockings off with his teeth and take her right away, but the game would be over much too soon and she wanted to be handcuffed first. He thought it best to play the game until the end, or otherwise the ride home would be full of argument and tension. His eyes became fixated even further as she undid the white cotton blouse she was wearing, lifting it above her head and off, leaving it beside her skirt on the forest floor.

He gasped at the sheer magnitude of her sexiness. Sensuality oozed from every pore of her skin and his gaze became fixated on the red basque she wore, accentuated with black lace trimmings around her stomach and breast area. Tonight her bust looked even bigger and he felt a primal urge within, which sent signals to his manhood, making it grow and thicken with a ferocious intensity. Jessica reached a hand out to touch it, but Rick batted the hand away, making her pull a sorry face. He laughed and pointed a finger to her to lean against the tree trunk.

"Your Lord commands you to lean against this tree. He is going to ravish you until you explode. He will devour every part of your body and work you until you are desperate to end the game. As your Lord and master you cannot disobey his orders and must do as he says! Do you understand wench?!!"

Rick pushed her against the tree and forced both her arms above her head. He slapped the handcuffs on both wrists, which forced them to remain in the air, allowing him the full view of her hourglass figure and the ability to turn her around if he wished. Rick pressed himself hard against her, forcing his tongue into her mouth, which sent a tingling sensation down her entire body, reaching her sex. She felt her nipples hardening and she squealed as he then moved his mouth to her breasts, sucking her nipples through the fabric of the basque. She wriggled with excitement as he dropped to the ground on both knees and she felt his tongue probing against her sex.

"I won't stop until you're shaking Jess and screaming my name. I want to be all you think about when you wake up in the morning and before you go to sleep at night. I want to take over your dreams. You will be mine forever my slave, bound to me forever."

Jessica felt Rick's hand sliding up her left thigh until it reached her sex. She screamed as both Rick's hand and tongue probed it from the outside, first gentle strokes and then firm strokes, like a cat lapping at it's milk.

"God Rick, put me out of my misery and shove it in me for Christ's sake! I can't wait much longer!!!" she said, shoving her sex onto Rick's hand and tongue.

"That would be too easy wench! I am the master, you are the slave. My wish is your command. Now turn around and face the tree bitch! Now!!! Hurry up and do what I say before I make you bleed!!!"

Rick's voice boomed, scaring an owl in the tree, which flew off in a hurry.

Jessica turned around. The sight of her enveloped Rick with lustful desire to force himself upon her. He leant into her and she could feel him probing against her buttocks and she gasped as he placed light kisses on the back of her neck, feeling her red basque being removed. The rain hammered against her soft skin, sending shivers throughout her body. Rick proceeded to kiss her from one shoulder to the next and she felt his tongue travel down her back until it reached just above her black panties. Biting onto them he pulled them down until they fell to the forest floor.

She screamed as he entered her from behind. Every stroke felt as if she was being played like the strings on a guitar. He took it slow at first, but as he sped up his hands reached for her breasts, grasping them tightly as he continued to thrust back and forth. Rick felt himself coming close with every thrust. He didn't want to disappoint her so early, but the sensation throughout his whole body was telling him otherwise. He felt himself explode, endorphins coursing through every vein of his body, reaching his head and filling him with elation. He moved out of her and she screamed in ecstasy as she felt his hand moving up her thighs, fingers entering her, toying with her emotions, like a puppeteer playing with their puppet.

"Oh God yes! Rick, oh yes!" she screamed. A waterfall erupted from her and splashed against the brown leaves on the forest floor. Soon she felt she could not give up any more, but he stroked her again and again, until she flowed like a river. When it started to hurt, she asked him to stop and being a gentleman he did.

"I love you Jess. Let's get into the car and drive home! We do have a party to attend you know." Rick said, taking her by the hands. He unlocked the handcuffs and removed them.

They were about to make their way to the front of the car, when they heard a rustling of leaves from the dense forest. Jessica screamed as five robed men in hoods rushed her and Rick, forcing them both to the ground. Rick managed to punch one of the men, but the others held him down, beating him until he lost consciousness. Jessica, got up and headed to the front, hoping she could grab the baseball bat she kept just in case someone tried to enter the car when she was stuck at traffic lights. As she reached the front, she was met by another hooded figure in a red robe, who removed their hood and revealed who they were.

"Hello sis!" Ronnie said smiling. Jessica, confused, was lost for words for a moment. When she attempted to speak she felt herself falling into unconsciousness, as a pair of hands grasped her around the throat, squeezing until she fell to the forest floor again.

JESSICA SLOWLY OPENED her eyes as she regained consciousness. She went to move forward, but struggled to move as her legs and arms were bound to an ornately carved wooden chair, which was fit for a king or queen. The rain had stopped and she noticed she had been dressed in a long flowing white robe which although see through seemed to shield her from the cold night air. Her first thought was to look where Rick was, as he had been beaten to what looked like a pulp. Her face dropped and she let out an anguished gasp as she looked upon the sad form of Rick, who has been hoisted onto a cross, splayed out in the form of Christ at the crucifixion. His hands were tied rather than nailed in, which was a slight relief to her, He had been placed in white briefs and she looked at the word which had been carved into his chest with a knife: PIG. His face and arms were scored with hundreds of lacerations, where they had continuously whipped him and his chest was also full of bruises. He had been punched so many times that his skin had started to blister and weep. As she began to weep, Ronnie appeared from the shadows in her red hooded robe and started to speak.

"My friends! It is a great night indeed in which power can be bestowed upon us by our dark Lord. In recognition of us providing him with the flesh of my sister and her pig, it is likely he will provide us with more power than we could ever imagine. On this Samhain, we ask our Lord to be gracious and to guide us to a better path. A path that leads us to his kingdom, the underworld of hell. Prepare the pig! We need to drink from him!!!"

Ronnie snapped her fingers at two robed figures who proceeded to take their athames and sharpen them against a stone before making their way towards Rick. Two stools were placed for them to stand on and Rick screamed in excruciating pain as they cut away at his chest in the shape of an upside down cross. The cross of St. Peter. They laughed with glee as the blood gushed from his stomach and cascaded onto them like a shower of rain, and licked the blood wine from their lips as it trickled down their foreheads towards their hungry mouths. Both of them caressed Rick's legs and started to kiss each other to feel the warm thickness of his blood coursing through their veins.

"Enough of this! Bring the pig's body so we can drain it of blood to toast the resurrection of our Lord! He will be most pleased at our offering to him. He has waited so long to quench his lust, he has started to get an appetite."

Ronnie beckoned a further two robed figures to do her bidding, who proceeded to cut away at the bindings on Rick's hands and feet. He screamed in agony as they yanked him off the upside down cross. Pointing at the stone slab before her, Ronnie's eyes lit up with a fiery intensity which betrayed her envy of Jessica and Rick's strong relationship, which she had now managed to bring to an end. Jessica winced as they slammed Rick's body against the slab, with such force that his stomach split completely open, oozing blood from the now wide opening.

"Get the black chalice and hold it to the opening. The wine of the pig is ours to drink. Soon He will be amongst us and we shall rejoice. Get the girl ready. Our Lord will be wanting to taste her very soon and she obviously looks like a bitch sloth. I have some makeup by the altar. Untie her but be forceful, so she doesn't escape and make her look ravishing. If she doesn't we will indeed feel His wrath. Hurry! Quick! We haven't got long until it reaches dawn and then it's likely He won't appear at all. All we need is for someone to spy on us and report us to the authorities and we'll be shut down!"

Jessica sobbed as the robed figures pressed on Rick's stomach forcing the blood to flow into the chalice, this being replaced by another chalice, and then finally a third, which only filled half way. A lot of his blood had trickled onto the forest floor and was not recoverable as it had drained away into the soil. She felt the bonds tying her to the chair being removed and strong hands hoisted her from it, carrying her to the black altar, where she was dropped ungraciously on top of it.

This she thought was the ideal time to make a run for it.

"Don't think about it bitch! One move and I'll slice those pretty lips off your face and eat them! Be good and you get to sleep with our Lord. Oh I wish I could sleep with him myself, but it's not allowed."

Jessica felt a blade against her neck. The robed figure who spoke to her removed their hood. It was Ronnie's friend Trish.

What the hell is going on she thought.

The blade moved from her neck and cut away at the cloth binding her mouth shut. Soon it was off and she was able to speak.

"Trisha what the hell is going on? Is this some sort of joke at my expense? Rick's not hurt at all is he? This is some sort of Halloween prank on me right?"

Jessica looked at Trisha for answers, with a puzzled expression of anguish and confusion. Trisha shook her head with a stern no.

"Jess, you are to be the Lord's for him to do with as he wishes. There's no telling what form he will appear in to you. He could appear as a blond haired, blue eyed hunk, but in the same breath, he could appear in his actual form. You know who Satan is right?"

Jessica felt makeup being applied to her face and lipstick being drawn on her mouth. She felt clothed under the robe, which she untied. She had been placed in a black bra and satin briefs with black stockings. Although she looked extremely alluring, she felt sick. Rick was in danger and she was at risk of being ripped apart by one of the most evil beings to ever exist. If indeed he did.

Satan was the stuff of myth surely she thought.

Some would argue that without Satan there would be no God and without evil there cannot be good.

"I know who Satan is Trisha. He's God's arch enemy. A sometimes suave and manipulative person who offers you the world in return for your soul, when you die. You can be living a life of luxury and decadence one minute and then screaming as you burn in hell the next. In my opinion, he is one of the most gluttonous beings ever to exist, only interested in his own well being and willing to use any means necessary to get what he wants. I certainly won't be sleeping with him if and when he shows up. I'd rather die first!"

Jessica spoke with a strong steadfast attitude, meaning every word. She was startled when Ronnie begun to start shouting.

"Gather round all witches here,
You have nobody, nothing to fear,
For He is coming, Our Lord Satan,
To have my sister for the taking,
In pay we'll live our wildest dreams,
Whilst hearing Jess' wildest screams,
So charge your chalices, drink and share
For he is here so be aware!
Espretu, norfana, morticus, althain,

Mordred, Lectivius, Armana, Yethane,
Be not frightened, His name proclaim,
Our Lord Satan is here again!!!"

As Ronnie chanted another group of hooded black robed figures appeared. Jessica counted how many there now were. 13! A witches coven! Ronnie was not joking about. He was coming!

"Satan, our Lord come! Charge your chalices, His will be done!"

As Ronnie chanted again, the chalices were passed around so all could drink Rick's blood. Some had to have the chalices taken away from them, as they were relishing the warm taste of blood too much. A cold chill filled the air and a freezing breeze spread through the forest, travelling to the altar. She smelt a sulphuric smell which seemed to travel around her. She felt her robe being removed by an unknown force, scalding hands touching her legs, edging their way up to her black satin briefs. Yet when she looked there was nobody there. What was going on?

"Show yourself you vile goat! I am not allowing you anywhere near my body as you stink of the rotting flesh of a thousand men! You are nothing but a proud gluttonous sloth, who thinks they can have what they want. Well, you can't have me so fuck off!!!"

Jessica went to jump off the altar, but was held down by the invisible force, who she presumed was Satan. As she struggled she saw something materialising before her eyes. It was Rick!!!

"Oh Rick! I thought you were dead! They cut you open didn't they and drunk your blood! How are you alive and in front of me now? This doesn't make any sense at all."

Jessica felt Rick's strong hands move up her body to her black bra. They moved around the back and unfastened it, which he tossed to the forest floor. She felt his lips move to her left and right breasts, and she moaned as he started to suck on both nipples gently. She winced as he nipped them with his teeth. His tongue moved to her mouth, forcing it open, allowing it to slip inside, which sent signals down to her sex yet again. She wanted him now, just as always, but wasn't he dead? Was this a trick? Satan was a trickster after all.

"Jess, you're so beautiful. I want to spend the rest of my life with you. Grow old and have children with you. Say you'll be mine forever until the end of time. Please say you mean it."

As Rick said the words, his eyes glowed a fiery red and yet they were as black as coal. He forced his tongue again in her mouth, their tongues met and she tasted the bitter salty taste of lust and love.

She moaned as he reached his hands to her black panties and peeled them off. He was quick with his attack, entering her with a ferocity which she had never experienced before. He grasped her round the throat with his left hand and as she struggled for breath his thrusts increased in intensity and he begun to growl like a wounded wolf, looking for it's mate in the wilderness.

"I..don't know...what's come over you...Rick...You're never this forceful. Urgh!" she cried in anguish as she could feel herself flowing again. This time with more waves than she'd ever experienced before. Her eyes rolled back in ecstasy, but this time they rolled back so far she felt as if she were looking at her innermost soul. Rick never had such power over her normally. How was he able to tonight? she thought.

"Jess, tell me you love me, want me and desire me like no other and you will serve as my queen for eternity. I need you by my side to rule over all and we can show them such pain and pleasure together. What do you say, my sweet Jess?"

Rick curled his lips and revealed his perfect white teeth. His incisors looked sharper than usual.

"This is taking role play to a new level Rick. You even got Ronnie involved and she did a star turn tonight. Bravo to you both and all the cast." she said, honestly believing that they had created their very own horror movie to celebrate Halloween Night.

"I'll do anything to please you babe, and you'll do anything to please me too won't you babe? I can give you the world if you'll just say you'll be mine forever. We can go to places you've never been to before, as long as you swear to serve me for all time. Swear it, swear it, swear it!" Rick said thrusting at her again. She was about to declare her undying love and devotion to him when she heard him calling her name from the direction of the stone slab.

"How is that possible?" she spoke aloud, pushing Rick aside so she could see in the direction where his other voice was coming from.

"Jess, help me! Please help me! I can't move and I feel like I'm drifting away. What the fuck is happening to me? Help me please!"

Rick's screams echoed through the forest. She leapt off the altar and ran to where she found Rick, his stomach slit open as before. His eyes were as white as the robe she was wearing and his skin was grey, with flashes of red where he had been flogged so many times. She wept as she realized Satan had tricked her. Her sister had been in on it as well. A sick revenge for not being able to have Rick for herself. She cradled Rick's head against her naked chest and spoke soothingly to him until she felt his life force leave his body. She began to sob uncontrollably but was abruptly stopped by her sister's shrill voice.

"Rejoice all! The cunt pig is dead! His bitch has been defiled and is now promised to our Lord. We are just a step away from fulfilling all our dreams and fantasies. Take the cunt pig away and bury him deep in the forest. The dawn will soon be here and we need to make haste and leave! Hurry up! Go! Go!!"

Ronnie made her way to Satan, but he seemed disinterested in someone who would literally throw themselves at him. He wanted Jessica. She was a more fiery feast to behold.

"Ronnie. Thank you for the gift of your sister to me. She will make the most suitable Lady of Hell and I'm sure will sire many fine children for me. It's about time we had some new demi-demons down there! What did you want anyway? How much power do you desire? Speak to me!"

Satan sneered and a puff of smoke rose from his lips as he spoke.

"My Lord, surely you need a wife who can fulfill your needs in all departments? Jess can fulfill your carnal needs, but you will soon be bored of her, as she grows old and feeble. Surely I can give you all you desire, with an insatiable appetite for sex. The more depraved the better. I will do whatever you want, with who you want and what you want. You can still have your share of other women, as long as I am Queen! Say yes my Lord and I will give my all to you and more!!!"

Ronnie clung onto Satan, stroking his manly chest, finding his erect nipples and tweaking them, hoping this would get him aroused. Disinterested he moved away from her and over to Jessica.

"Stay away from me you evil bastard! He's dead. You all did this you sick fucks! What am I going to do without him? He's my life. I love him so much. No one could ever replace him. Stay away and fuck off!"

Jess screamed so loudly that a flock of birds flew in fright from a nearby oak tree. She hammered her fists against Satan's chest, which had no effect on him at all. He smiled at her sarcastically and then he begun to roar with a mighty wrath. Most of the coven of witches fled, knowing that he was displeased and that if they got in his path he would smite them down and damn them to an eternity of being bound and gagged in hell, to burn at his pleasure.

Ronnie however was not scared of him. She rushed at him with her athame, plunging it in his back. He howled, but she screamed as he turned around and spat venomous flames from his mouth, scarring her skin as they touched her, pussy boils appearing and bursting everywhere. He grasped her by the head and lifted her up, pressing both hands on either side of it, causing her skull to implode. Her brain exploded, splattering all over his face, which was now also drenched in the puss and blood. He reached behind his back for the athame and pulled it out without a care in the world. Moving towards Jessica he lunged at her throat, shaking her ferociously. The force of this caused her to bang her head against the forest floor and she lost consciousness.

JESSICA WOKE UP IN her bed. She lifted the blanket away from herself to see what she was dressed in. She was wearing a white bra and panties, which definitely wasn't what she was wearing last night? Poor Rick! She had to phone the police to inform them of his murder. Would they believe her, especially seeing as last night was Halloween?

"So you're finally up then?" said Rick appearing in the bedroom doorway, naked except for a pair of red satin boxer shorts, tight enough to expose the huge bulge in them. He gave her a seductive wink and made his way to the bed. Seduction was clearly on his mind.

"Stop right there! Have you forgotten last night? I saw you murdered in cold blood! My sister was in on it too and Satan tore her apart and crushed her skull in! It's not you is it Rick? It's bloody Satan! Stay away from me! Stay away!!!"

Jessica made a run for the kitchen, rifling through the drawers until she found a bread knife. She felt it's serrated edges to make sure it was sharp enough to do him harm. Taking the knife, she made her way back to the bedroom, but was startled when the front door bell rang. She made her way to answer the door, opening it slightly ajar, knife still in her right hand.

"Hi Sis! I just thought I'd come round to check how you were. Rick told me you were asleep before you even had the chance to come round last night? You missed a fantastic party! Let me in please!" Ronnie said, pushing slightly at the door,

"Okay, but I'm not dressed yet!" Jessica said, opening the door.

Ronnie stepped in, wearing a black t-shirt and black leather trousers. The bra she wore pushed her breasts up so high, it looked as though they would spill out of her t-shirt.

Rick came out of the bedroom, but was now fully dressed. He looked at Ronnie with disdain, his eyes glowing fiery red to warn her to keep her distance and to keep her mouth shut.

"I must have had a really bad dream last night. Rick was dead and you had your skull crushed in by the devil! Did I have anything to drink last night Rick?", Jessica said, hiding the knife behind the coat rack she had placed beside their bedroom.

"Nothing more than usual beautiful." Rick said.

Jessica moved towards him, cuddling him and he gave her a gentle kiss.

"I'm just going to use your bathroom Sis", Ronnie said, making her way into it and locking the door.

She looked in the mirror and saw the true vision of herself, charred skin with no lips, fragments of her crushed skull visible between the burnt matted shreds of hair she had left. She sobbed as she realized the huge mistake she had made. It wouldn't be too long until Jessica realized she was living in Hell and that all she saw was an illusion. Ronnie wanted to tell her, but Satan had advised against telling her sister or Jessica would suffer the same fate as her.

Outside Jessica was feeling relieved. It had all been a bad dream. She still had her Rick and her sister was being very nice for once to him too. It couldn't be much better she thought.

"Rick, let's celebrate Halloween tonight! We could visit Hawkswood Forest and have some fun alone. Ronnie won't stay the whole day!"

Jessica kissed him and they held each other for what felt like an eternity in a lingering embrace.

As they kissed, Satan saw Ronnie standing in the bathroom doorway. He sneered at her again and she proceeded to make her way back into the bathroom, closing the bathroom door. She started to sob once she turned the taps on, so Jessica couldn't hear her.

Finishing their kiss, he began to speak to Jessica.

"Of course we can! What's the worst thing that can happen? Happy belated Halloween beautiful!", he said and as she turned away for a second his eyes glowed with an intense fire to them. Tonight would be killer, he thought, smiling to himself.

# Jason White

Jason White is the author of The Fridge, The Possession Of Clearwater Falls and Season Of The Dead. His short stories have been featured in the horror anthologies Holiday Horror and Night Mares. He has also contributed additional writing to the short film Beer Cellar, part of the Blaze Of Gory Anthology DVD. Additionally he is featured in the Blaze Of Gory screenplay book and Bloody Hell - The Making Of Blaze Of Gory book.

Please connect with Jason if you wish to collaborate with him via social media:

Facebook: @officialjasonwhiteauthorpage
Twitter: @JasonJayWhite
Instagram: @jasonwhitehorrorauthor
E-mail: **jtawhite@hotmail.com**

# Blood Will Out
## Katie Jaarsveld

From the beginning, there was an unrest. Too many creators with their own ideals. There was only one commonality, Angels. They weren't created, they were simply there. For all the creators knew, angels could have created them.

The angels were aware of this, and they wanted what they were due, while the creators demanded that they were the rightful rulers. Continually challenging the creators started a war among the angels. They were split among the decisions within themselves.

Swords were drawn and the war of the angels began. Man could feel the earth shake and vibrate, but it came from under their feet. As swords clashed, man saw lightning and heard thunder. The rains upon their heads came in torrents, starting plagues and sickness.

What was referred to as tears or rain was in all actuality, angel's blood. The sun dried it, but it did nothing to help water animals or man's crops. Animals who drank the angels blood became sterile and the meat was vile. Crops burst into flames at harvest.

Water from the land itself was plentiful, and when used, it healed the lands, animals and man.

The war continued for a time unknown.

What had started as a war among angels soon became a war within man. The fallen angels became saints, while man was given rules and guidelines on what was or was not permissible. The angels had been gifted a talent or responsibility along with their wings, which the fallen angels sacrificed. Their talents were torn from them just as if their skin was ripped away. Their wings were part bone. Yes, even angels had a type of flesh and bone, just different than mans.

For the angel's wings to be removed, the feathers were pulled from the skin, and bones had to be broken, taking decades of torture. After losing their talents, all that remained was flesh filled with pain. Only after the wings were removed were they allowed to surrender their immortality and let Death himself take them. For without souls, they ceased to exist, except in memories.

There were seven virtues bestowed on seven who had proven themselves to be honorable over time. Out of all mankind, only seven were deemed worthy post-angel wars, death, disease and famine. The seven respected their given talents for a time. Whether it was decades or centuries was not known. As the Earth revolved, man evolved, changing and forgetting or compromising their worthiness.

The seven grew bored with their talents and the rules that came with them. They wanted to see the world and experience the wholeness of their talents. They had been warned of a side of their talent that they were not to use. But why not? They had all been entrusted with talents and they should all be able to explore them to the fullest extent.

That was fine. But as we all know, over time, people, beliefs and convictions were replaced. Whether they become more with their convictions or lose them altogether, but rarely do people stay the same. The way life, people and the world were, change was inevitable.

It was a slow process, as were many of them, the change from virtue to sin. There had to be something which triggered the ultimate negative emotion.

HUMILITY WAS HUMBLE above all else, and yet, he still made up one being. Without him, others wouldn't be who they were, for he was the first in creation. It was in his knowledge that others would not exist without him.

Humility stripped its soul, ripping the skin apart until he surrendered his being humble. The outcome was a vane one and could not change back to the way it had been, even if the soul wasn't damaged and tattered. The soul withered and blew as the wind. As a result the soul could not be found and placed back in its core.

Humility had given so much of its very being, that when all was said and done, there was a brief regret. But the switch had been flipped, bringing about the change, to never return as it once was.

The vanity of someone who believed in humility was replaced by pride. Humility and pride were the states of virtues of what made up a being. While one was considered to be the best virtue, the other was the worst of the sins, known for consuming its host.

For without the meekness to ask for help or to surrender to itself, pride engulfed what good remained. The soul was ripped from its human connection, inflicting pain that not even angels could deem imaginable. Twisting and changing, torturing itself until it was no longer recognizable, becoming a thing that no longer knew itself. After humility fell, the others felt a sense of loss.

Even in knowing they would change and maybe cause irreparable damage to themselves, the remaining six decided as a collective to explore what the other half of their talent would change them into. They had already given up their individuality, deciding the seven would remain intact at whatever the cost.

From that day, humility was only pride.

KINDNESS WAS THE SECOND to explore its talent. He held an admiration for the spirit and was admired almost as much as forgiveness. While one creator believed you could not exist without a heart, it was argued the same could be said of the spirit. With the continual bickering, he was overwhelmed with jealousy and became enveloped by Envy. Though it was no fault of its own, as it was learned by example.

One creator told of the beauty of the heart, as kindness possessed. Another suggested the spirit was where kindness excelled and glowed in beauty.

For a kind one, admired by all for its inner beauty and grace, it wasn't enough. Its jealousy was all-consuming. It ate at his heart until you couldn't recognize the beauty it once possessed. An immortal could live without a heart, just as an empty shell.

The spirit withdrew, for without a heart, you possessed no beauty at all.

Of course, the creators blamed others for a lack of kindness and his beauty, not accepting or recognizing their part in him no longer remaining.

Being kind wasn't always enough. You were expected to possess an outer beauty. Of course, if you didn't contain the inner beauty, then you would crave it. The memory of the kindness of the spirit was only remaining in the eyes of envy.

TEMPERANCE WAS OF SELF-restraint to keep the body clean. For all of its self-restraint, he fell into a drunkenness of appetite and self-indulgence. Its motto simply became, *more*. There was no limit to its demands and developed into gluttony. The appetite became insatiable for more than just food.

It extended itself into items of wealth or symbols of status.

He failed to do the one thing required, to take care of the body. With his limitless appetite, his virtue was no longer a restraint.

There was always more to taste, drink and he over-indulged in it all. It came to the day that he could no longer move from his sickening, bloated body. His skin had stretched beyond the limits of its elasticity, and started to tear. Small, insignificant rips at first, in the folds of his flesh. Stretch marks were gaping open, spilling its contents. And still, he didn't stop.

Only after his face and throat were so swollen that he could not take another bite, did he stop. Because when his throat closed, there was no breath. While one could survive without some pieces as immortals, air was not one of them.

He had found a pleasure in consuming everything, changing from temperance to the loathed gluttony.

CHARITY HAD ALL OF the giving from mind and self, and was a giving one without end. He could not do enough for others. Over time, greed took control of the mild manner, developing a need for power, money and possessions.

Charity was giving of himself and his possessions until there was nothing left for him.

Of all, his sin took over more slowly, as it was his way to give, and not consider himself as much. It progressed so gradual, that he actually felt good about the change, and in that he was still taking care of others. Until he wasn't.

The weight of his mind was causing headaches until the pressure needed to be relieved. Sores were producing under his hair, with bumps that oozed. When he squeezed them to relieve the pressure, the bump would enlarge, causing more pressure.

His mannerisms changed shortly after. He took without provocation, demanded that *it was his* by his own right of mind. With his mentality changed, his body took over in punishing him for his deeds. The more he took, his hands blistered with sores that opened. They spread over his body, suffocating him, as it was his punishment for exploiting his virtue.

He had found that in order to not have to repeatedly start over, he needed to be less charitable and be filled with greed.

CHASTITY WAS KNOWN for its purity; therefore he protected himself against a tarnished body.

He was purity in every form.

What had started off as experimenting with his virtues to taste the sin, he found there was so much to learn that he committed himself to gathering as much knowledge about the pleasures as he could. Then it was time to push his knowledge forth to serving his sin.

Partners, positions and toys weren't enough.

He became consumed with his extreme sexual lust. Until he found such a sexual electricity within himself and became excessive, with an appetite that could not be quenched.

The skin started peeling off in an attempt to cleanse itself. The more he peeled off, the more there was to remove, as it was the only way to stop the itching.

His heart exploded from his escapades, not being able to withstand the betrayal of going from pure to lust driven.

In chastity's loss of pureness, he lost his heart as well, having it felt as if it had been scratched from his chest. As the penance it actually was, as chastity ceased to exist; only lust remained.

DILIGENCE WAS FOUND to possess a zeal for integrity, to learn life and labor. After a time, life happened and the drive to keep going suffered. With its idleness, the mind grew lazy from lack of use, and with it, the laziness grew until it wanted nothing. Even breathing could be perceived as a hard task.

The virtue he had been honored with had made his mind sharp. He was well-liked and appreciated.

Once he felt his sin, his brain started to dry and shrivel. The mind was only as good as its activity. When thoughts are squished and by-passed, the brain loses the thought process. Just as when you close a door, you cannot see the sunlight.

Losing one's' mind is as calming as it is painful. The things you cherished were the first to go. While the thoughts that brought pain, tortured you to the end, and beyond.

Diligence found his idleness of mind had turned him to sloth.

FORGIVENESS HELD COMPOSURE in the heart, and felt emotions with an intenseness. When he faltered, the positive emotions also faltered, leaving anger to writhe in its wrath.

The last was forgiveness, with its composure to release vengeance and resentments. At some point, you have to say, *enough* or become overwhelmed. Such an anger you cannot keep pushing down without the consequences of such a strong emotion overriding the calmness you once possessed.

He witnessed the virtues changed to sins, and the change of six of his comrades. In each ones turn, he forgave them for giving in, their actions, and for leaving the rest alone, to remember the one before them.

What he could not forgive, was the manner that the creators deemed that his companions suffer to die. He felt no calm within himself after the sixth died, leaving him alone.

When forgiveness could no longer feel the calm of his heart, all that was left was his wrath.

He cursed the others, himself, and mostly the creators. They knew man was weak and his capabilities. Were the seven a test to each other or to punish the angels or man? Maybe all of them.

His madness gripped every negative emotion he could summon. He woke the angels and creators alike. For his rantings, he would receive the harshest punishment of all. He would endure *all* punishments. At once.

The pain he was consumed by made even Death himself cringe. Screaming during it all, until he could not speak through the pain.

His soul was stripped and tortured, his heart squeezed flat and the spirit ripped from his body. He couldn't breathe, and felt his mind slip away with anything good, leaving behind the things which tortured the whole being. While being covered in painful sores that increased pressure as they grew. The peeling of his skin while his heart was shredded, simultaneously. The only release was when his brain dried, to leave him some quiet.

Only after that was his immortality released by the creators, so Death could deal with the remnants as he had with the six before.

THERE WERE SEVEN UNPARDONABLE sins and would not be forgiven, instilling fear in those who would possess the virtuous talents. It was decided by the creators that all sins weren't deadly, just the chosen seven.

Haughty eyes produced sin and left a soul without wisdom. A lying tongue was deceitful with the will and desire to lie. The shed of innocent blood would initiate harm, and shall cause a life for a life, a wound for a wound. A wicked heart enjoys others misfortunes, controls, manipulates and holds no moral compass. Haste for evil leads to a swiftness for violence. False witness reflects negatively on another's character being judged. For one who initiates discord among others, they will be dealt strife.

If women had been given the talents, I have no doubt it would have turned out differently. For women would have tried to integrate both sides from the beginning.

Everything which was good had become the harshest of what would be known as the seven deadly sins. Pride, Envy, Gluttony, Greed, Lust, Sloth and Wrath.

*end*

# Katie Jaarsveld

Katie lives in the Netherlands with her husband, dwarf pinscher Jubjub and 2 cats, Scout and Jack.

When not spending time with her husband, pets, family and friends, she can be found engrossed in a favorite book, reviewing an author's latest release, or most importantly, writing her next bestseller.

Katie started by writing horror, and though that is still her favorite genre, she has also released stories in contemporary, paranormal, supernatural, fantasy, mythopoeia, young adult, and even romance.

Twitter @katiejaarsveld

Facebook **https://www.facebook.com/marytink.w**

# All Seven
# Samie Sands
# Wrath

Once upon a time, I was a normal girl in love with a normal guy. At least, I thought I was. Little did I know Lewis had a side-chick who was about to ruin everything.

If only I'd seen it coming, maybe I wouldn't be here now.

If only I wasn't so trusting, I wouldn't have had my little *accident*.

If only I didn't love so much, maybe I could've recovered from this like a normal person.

*If only.*

There's a reason rage is always represented as red, and it's the blood. Anger comes with a lot of blood, as I now know.

"Now what?"

The blood drips onto the floor, making a real mess of things. Just more for me to clean up. Stupid really. I've got other things to focus on.

Like the dead body.

"Damn it."

I grab my cell phone and call the one person responsible for this. He has to help me because none of this would've happened if not for him.

"Hey, Polly." Asshole. He sounds much too happy. "What's going on? What're up to?"

"Meet me at Melinda's house."

"Melinda?" I can't help getting a bolt of satisfaction when the name makes him go all weird. "Why would I meet you there?"

"You know why. Because I found out the truth about you and her. So, I suggest you get your ass here, and now."

I hang up before he can argue. I don't want to listen, don't want to hear what he has to say.

Little fucker. Has no idea who he's up against.

Blackness swirls through me, combines with the red, prepares to clean up the mess left behind once Lewis is gone too. I can't let him live when poor bitchy Melinda had to die just for falling for his charms. There needs to be a balance, it has to make sense.

Black magik is useless otherwise. *He* didn't give me dark magik just to create chaos.

See, most people think *He* wants chaos but it isn't like that at all. It's balance. I accidently got rid of Melinda because she made me so mad, but since it's all Lewis's fault, *He* will want him as well.

No other way.

"Don't worry, little Melinda," I whisper into her cold, dead ear. "I'm going to kill him too.

Im 'iens ut interficias eum. You don't need to worry. His bad deed will be punished just as much as yours."

She rises from the floor and flings around the room like a rag doll. It's hard to imagine there was ever any life inside of there. She's a pretty shell, sure, but with nothing inside, what's the point?

"You could've become something, little Melinda, had you not screwed around with my guy. What a shame you messed around with the wrong person."

Weirdly, there's something about her dead body which fascinates me, sparks desire in me, makes me yearn for me. I might've possessed black magik my whole life, but this is the first time I've used it for death. It feels good.

*I* feel good. More powerful than I ever have done before.

"Polly!"

Oh shit, Lewis has no idea about my powers...oh, well I guess he
does now.

"Polly, what the hell are you doing?"

Melinda splats on the floor with a thump. Blood ricochets everywhere.

"What have you done?" Lewis is pale with terror. Good. "What did
you do to Melinda? What the hell were you doing just then? How did
you...you get her up in the air like that? It isn't right..."

"But you screwing around with her behind *my* back was okay, was
it?"

"I don't know what you're talking about."

"Oh yes you do. Don't lie, Lewis. I *know* about the pair of you. I
know about all of it. So, you might as well be honest with me. Tell me
what you did."

Why isn't he looking at me? Why is he fixated on that dead bitch?
She's gone now. She can't *still* win.

"Oi, Lewis, you nasty piece of work. Can you focus on what's important here, huh? Or don't you like living?"

That's enough to get him staring at me.

"Oh, that's right, Lewis. I'm not afraid to kill you as well."

"You...you don't need to do that." Now he's scared, even more so.
Good. "You don't need to kill me. I might have made a mistake, Polly,
but I won't do it again. It was Melinda, really. She's the one who came
onto me. She made herself basically impossible to resist and I was foolish. But believe me, I've learnt my lesson now. It won't happen again."

Ooh I like listening to him beg. I could get used to this. Unfortunately, I know he's lying. I know more than he thinks I do.

"You promise?" I tuck my finger underneath his chin, forcing him
to look me in the eyes. "I would like to believe you, you know? That
you won't ever cheat on me again. But isn't there a saying?" I cock my
head to one side. "Once a cheat, always a cheat."

"N...not me. Not me, I swear it, Polly. I love you. I see that now. I didn't realize it before because I'm an idiot. But you've shown me the truth. I see it now. I want you. Only you."

I let him kiss me. I let his lips meet mine like I'm not flooded with so much anger I can't contain it. I let him believe that for just a second, every will be okay...

But then I reach deep into his chest and I yank his heart free. His pulsing bloody heart. Lewis stares at it in shock, as if he can't believe that I've physically done to him the same as he did to me.

"I wanted to be a normal girl for you, Lewis. I wanted to stop using black magik so me and you could be together. But you've reminded me of the truth. Humans are weak, idiotic, a slave to their emotions. *I* am a million times better than you. So, now it's time for me to go out there and embrace who I am, to kill like I'm supposed to. Thank you for that."

"P...Polly." He staggers backwards, blood pouring from his chest. "Polly, how could you?"

I can practically feel his blood pouring into me, giving me strength, pushing me forwards towards my destiny.

"I had to." I shrug one shoulder. "*He* wants you gone, I'm sure of it. You wronged me, so you need to die."

His eyes pop wide as he finally caves and falls to the floor with a thump next to his gross side-chick. I hope she was worth it. I'm glad the last thing he saw before death was me, it'll be a delightful memory for him to take into the afterlife with him.

Who knows, maybe Lewis will even watch me from down there as he's being tortured. Maybe he'll see me as I step into my destiny at long last, as I become the full-time killer I've always been destined to become...

# Lust

I didn't mean to find myself here with him, I just wanted him for myself, that's all. I can't help who I fall for and how I choose to express that love.

"Why are you doing this?"

"What's going to happen to me?"

"Are you going to let me go?"

All questions I can't answer. Not that he gets it.

Worst thing is it didn't need to be this way. He could've just given me a chance. He could've just been mine. It could've been so damn easy.

Is now the right time to kiss him? It seems strange to share our first kiss when he's tied up, but it could be sexy...

"I think you know what we're doing here." I circle him, my finger trailing delicately along his cheek. "Because it's time for you to notice me at last."

"N...notice? I notice you..."

"Oh no." I shake my head hard. No way I'm falling for that line now. "No, you don't, Wyatt. You walk passed me in the school hallway every single day and don't even glance at me. You always have a string of cheerleaders hanging off your neck, so why would you look at me there? But you're gunna look at me now, that's for sure."

"I see you, L...Linda..."

"Lydia."

What an asshole.

What a beautiful asshole.

"Lydia, right, sorry. I didn't mean to get your name wrong, I'm just a little freaked out, that's all. This is all so new to me. I've never been...you know, kidnapped before."

"This is love, Wyatt. Not kidnap. You might want to be a bit more careful with your words, because once I turn on the charm..."

I give him a little glimpse, adoring the way his face goes slack with need. Of course he wants me when my succubus powers, but I'd prefer him to need me anyway. That way, he doesn't have to lose his soul for me.

They always end up losing their souls for me. It keeps *Him* happy, but leaves me miserable.

Wyatt's going to be different, he's going to fall in love with the person I am underneath the succubus.

"Wow, you really are a beauty, Lydia." Urgh, his voice has that annoying monotone quality to it. It doesn't belong to him right now. "How did I not notice you before? Untie me now, so I can kiss you."

A thick ball of desire fills my throat, it's hard to breathe when he's staring at me like that. All I want to do is untie him and get my spoils, but it isn't real. I can't unlock him until it's real.

"I spotted you a long time ago, Wyatt. Maybe the first day I started at this high school..."

"*This* high school? Have you been to many?"

"More than you can possibly imagine. It's one of the perks of being immortal...or down sides, depending on the school."

"I...immortal?"

The color drains from his cheeks.

"Yes, it means I love forever, and you could too...if you want to." I pause for dramatic effect. "You want to love me forever, Wyatt?"

He says nothing, yet his silence speaks volumes. I might have to turn on the charm just a little, in the beginning anyway.

"You *are* beautiful, Lydia." Good, it's working. "Intoxicating, actually. Why haven't we ever hooked up?"

"You know why."

I hook my finger underneath his chin and force him to become fascinated by my eyes.

"I want to be yours, Lydia." He's in a whisper now, unable to make sound. "I want to belong to you."

"Oh, you do. That's why you're here. You're already mine." My lips curl up into a smile. "That isn't the question anymore. Instead, we need to work out what happens next."

"Do I have a choice in the matter?"

I tap my chin thoughtfully, acting like I'm really considering this. If he's the fool I think he is, he'll fall for this act.

"Please, Lydia," he begs, falling head first into my trap. "Please, let me decide this with you. I want to come to some kind of solution with you. I know I belong to you now, but we can work together."

Oh, how I would love to believe that.

"So, I let you out now and there's no fuss, huh? No trying to escape or whatever? I'm not going to get any trouble?"

He shakes his head hard. Too hard.

"Okay, Wyatt, come on then. I'll untie you."

I lean down towards him and turn up the charm once more. He nearly falls forward with his desire for me. If only it were real. Just once I want it to be real.

"So, I'm going to let you out now." My lips are almost on his. He's shuddering with need. "And then me and you are going to have some fun."

I loosen him, just a tiny bit and he stiffens. I've dialed my powers down and I can see him losing interest in me, thinking I'm crazy, he can't think that, he mustn't. In my thousands of years roaming this realm, I haven't ever wanted anyone to really like me as I do Wyatt. There's just something about him...

"I don't know, Wyatt. I don't think you're ready for me yet."

He's intoxicating. He's drawn me in and captivated me. I can't express how much I *need* him to just like me.

He likes everyone else, so why not me? Why has it taken this extreme for him to see me?

"I am ready, Lydia, I am. You need to trust me..."

"But I don't. I don't trust you not to run as soon as I free you."

I always win. Why am I not winning here? It's unbecoming for a succubus not to win.

"I won't run. I won't. You don't even need to...turn on the charm or whatever you call it?"

My head snaps around to stare at him. How does he know? I might've called it charm, but he knows more. He knows too much.

"Who are you, Wyatt? What are you?"

"What am I?" He rises to his feet, the ties loosening all by themselves. "Oh, Lydia...someone like you should know *exactly* what I am. I'm the same as you, the male version of you, haven't you worked that out yet?"

His nice smile turns into an ugly smirk. Any attraction I had to him before simply melts away into nothingness.

"I worked it out as soon as I saw you. I *knew* what you were, but I've come across your kind before."

He steps closer to me, growing in size and exploding out of his shirt. Ice-cold fear grips me. This is wrong, it's gone all wrong.

"And I've killed your kind before because female succubuses are just...so annoying."

"What are you talking about?"

My powers are ebbing away, I can feel it happening by the second.

"What are you doing to me?"

"You really haven't ever met another one of *us* before, have you?" he chuckles as I slip out of my body like a snake shedding its skin. "Because this is how it works. It isn't just about sending human souls to *Him*. You're young and naïve if you still believe that. It's survival of the fittest, we are all in a war to become *His* most trusted help, and you're losing. It's your first battle and you're already losing."

No, this isn't right, it can't be right. How can this be the way of life and I know nothing about it leaving me with an unfair disadvantage, it isn't right.

Then again, *He* does like to play with his toys and that's what all of us are. Pawns in his chess game.

I just can't believe I'm going down so easy and I don't have the strength to fight back.

What a waste.

# Pride

Many people don't know the Black Market is a real place. It's more just a term, isn't it? It's one of those things that's taken on a life of its own, but the Black Market is all too real, and I'm in charge.

It's not for stolen cell phones though, or stupid things people *think* they need but don't want to pay full price for. Oh no, it's much more serious than that.

What we sell...if you don't know about it, you ain't living, and most people on this planet haven't seen life yet. Some won't, the entire time they're on this realm.

"What d'ya want?" This guy is sketchy. Must be his first time here. "Don't be shy. You can ask for what you want. No judgment here, that's for sure."

"A...a..." His eyes are everywhere but on me. Fucking amateur. "A gun. A weapon of some kind. Maybe a hit man, that might be better. I don't really want to do this myself."

Urgh, such a *human* request.

Death, sex, money...that's all they care about.

"I can get you a hit man." Might as well get rich off these idiots while also serving my master. "What method do you want? Is this a 'revenge best served cold' type of deal?"

"I..." He shrugs helplessly. "I don't know."

I roll my eyes. "Come on, man, you gotta give me somethin'. Let me know how you want this done. *He* always prefers a bit of a dramatic flair, but of course, it's up to you."

"*He*? Do you mean...?" The color drains from his face. "Oh no, do you mean...?"

"Who d'ya think makes all o' this possible?" I cock an eyebrow. "It don't just happen. Sure, I'm the one who runs it. But *He's* pullin' the strings."

"I don't think I want to do this now..."

He's backing away, terror gripping him. Time to make my move.

"You sure?" He doesn't like me up in his personal space which makes it all the more satisfying. "You sure you don't want someone dead? I might not come across enthusiastic about murder, but I can assure you, I am. I just like something exciting to get my teeth into."

He gasps in a couple of short sharp breaths, which answers my question for me. With a roll of my eyes, I grab a chunk of his neck between my teeth and tear the flesh away from his bones.

"Urgh, you taste like shit." Blood spits from my lips. Bad manners are a part of me. "Idiot, but now I see your memories. Now I know who you wanted killed. Your ex-wife and her new man. That's boring, Ian. Honestly, you should'a come down here with something better. Something special."

I always aspired to run the Black Market when I was a demon working in Hell, because I thought it'd be more thrilling. Unfortunately, humans are boring as shit. They never make anything fun for me.

I can't help it if I need a bit more excitement, can I?

Devouring his flesh only satisfies me for a few short moments though. It's nowhere near enough. I kick his body into the 'spare parts' pit, disgusted with myself for letting him go so easily.

Shit, this is all so pointless.

"Who's next?"

A sexy young woman sashays towards me. Now this is better. Woman who seek out the Black Market are often more inventive than men. I don't know what it is, I guess their minds work a little better.

This woman's twisted needs might be just what I need today.

"And, how exactly can I help you?" I purr. "What do you have in mind?"

"I want something a little...kinkier."

Immediately, I'm struck. I'm in, hook, line, and sinker. Whatever this is, it sounds fun.

"Ooh, okay, well I'm sure that's something I can help you with. You share everything."

Her finger grazes down my cheek. On my unholy skin, she feels like sandpaper, yet I kinda like it. She's so hot, it feels good.

"I don't know if you're ready to hear what I want yet." She leans in and nibbles on my bottom lips. "I don't know if you're ready for *me*."

"You have no idea what I'm ready for..."

She starts by peeling off my jacket. This woman, this *human* woman, doesn't seem disgusted as the material sticks to my ungodly skin. If anything, she seems delighted, more excited by the whole thing.

She's a sicko and I like it.

"Can I undress you too?" I murmur, desire thick in my tone. It isn't often I have someone coming straight at me like this. "I want to see you."

"Not yet. I need you first. I need to see all of you."

Perhaps I should be uncomfortable, this should be a red flag, but it isn't.

"There is something wild about you, isn't there? I guess that's how you ended up here, ruler of all the crazy shit."

"Crazy...sure."

"You don't sound too certain about that?" She sways closer to me and presses her still clothed body up against mine. "You don't love it?"

"I would love more..."

I forget I'm naked. I lose myself in my own mind for a change.

"The pride I felt for this job isn't there anymore. I don't feel on top o' the world when I'm doing it. I just feel like...like humans are idiots."

Is this a therapy session? I'm spilling my guts and I can't seem to stop.

"I should big the Big Don, king of the underground shit, but I'm just...just another one of his slaves."

"My slaves, huh? That's how you feel?"

"What?"

I step back. I need some distance now.

"I wouldn't want you to be unhappy. I don't need a Judas in my ranks. If you don't want to be here then you can be on the other side of the torture, my little Asmodeus. I don't mind where you are, but I need someone on the front line who wants to be here, and that isn't you."

For the first time ever, I get what I always thought would be the proudest moment in my life. I see *Him* in his true form. But *He* is horrifying, terrifying, disgusting even to me, so I'm willing to jump headfirst into the punishment *He* has waiting for me. It's better than looking at *Him*.

Or *Her* as the case may be...

# Gluttony

"Tastes good," my date tells me with a sweet smile playing on his lips. "You are one hell of a cook."

I'm sure he doesn't like it really, it must be a strange taste to him, not something he's used to, but he's so desperate to get me into bed he'll say whatever it takes.

That's what all guys are like these days, isn't it? With dating apps and plenty on offer, they can never be satisfied with just one woman.

Little do they know when they come to my house I'm the last woman they'll ever be with.

Once they have Jac, they never go back.

"Glad you like it." The coy act is sickening, but it's what this man needs. "There's plenty more. I always make too much."

"Ooh, well maybe we'll need it if I end up staying over." What an irritating wink he has. "If you want me to that is. Bill never overstays his welcome."

"Well, Bill, you are welcome here for as long as you like. I am really enjoying my date with you. It's been a long time coming. It feels like we've been online chatting for ages."

"Oh, I know, tell me about it. Been good getting to know you though."

I slide my chair closer to him, batting my lashes. He angles his body, wanting more, needing more, and boy he's gonna get it.

"I don't mean to sound forward," I whisper. "And this is something I never usually do, but I think there's something special here and I don't want to miss out on a golden opportunity. Maybe most love stories don't start with sex on the first date, but this could be different, couldn't it?"

He doesn't hear me mention love, only sex, and his eyes light up in delight.

Men, they are all the same.

"Oh, well it isn't something I normally do either," he lies. "But sure, we can..."

I don't let him finish his sentence, instead I grab him like the passion is too much for me and I can't hold it in any longer. Our lips mash together and I can feel this idiot growing more excited by the second.

I am too, but for a very different reason. One he'll find out soon enough.

I need their blood pumping, it makes everything a million times better for me. Hot fiery blood is like a drug to me, one that I can't get enough of. It's why I always get them all riled up.

"You want to see me?"

I pull back and edge my dress slightly up my legs with a delighted twinkle in my eye. One he misreads, thankfully.

"Oh God, of *course* I want to see you. Have you taken a look at yourself, Jac? You're the sexiest woman I've ever seen. When I came across your picture on the dating app...wow, and then you actually look like that in person! You're one of kind."

Oh, that I am!

"Well, let me show you myself then. You must be keen to see all of me."

Just one item of clothing off is all it takes for his jaw to go slack. Man, this is easy, almost too easy. I almost just want to suck him dry now and have done with it.

But as I've learned in the past, a little bit of patience goes a long way. A *long* way, so I need to keep this up for just a little while longer.

"Woah, you're unreal."

"You think?" I tease. "That is nice of you."

"You're gorgeous. The most beautiful woman I have ever laid eyes on."

*Hold it, wait a moment,* I warn myself. *Any minute now.*

I say nothing, but continue to strip until there's nothing covering me. I'm proud of my body, I look good and eat well, so much so that I don't even need to work out, and Bill is appreciative.

"Oh wow," he groans again. "You're incredible."

His eyes travel slowly downwards, pausing at my breasts before moving down some more. While he's distracted, I slide along the floor closer to him, until I can hook my arms gently around his neck.

"I can't believe you like me."

And then I take him.

I dig my teeth into the exposed skin of his throat and I suck hard. The blood pumping hard in his veins slides into my body, feeding me, bringing me back to life—well as much as a vampire can be considered alive—and I drain him.

He tastes good. I knew he would because I got him all riled up. This is why I have to turn them on, because it makes everything that much more satisfying.

"Oops." I giggle when I spot splashes of blood all over my chest. "What a messy eater."

Not that I mind the mess, of course. When I'm fed, I don't mind anything. It's the rest of the time I can get cranky.

Thank goodness for dating apps though, bringing the worst kind of men to me so I can drain them and use what's left to make a meal for the next man.

Human meat we can share, and most of them like the taste even if it isn't something they've experienced before. Or at least they pretend to in an attempt to get me into bed, which is good enough, I suppose. It works. It gets me what I want.

Hey, I do try to warn them that one you have Jac you never go back. None of them heed the warning like they should. I can't be blamed for that.

Can I?

"Well, Bill," I declare with a messy smile as his weighty body slumps to the floor. "Thank you for a wonderful evening. I really got my satisfaction with you. And you will make a *great* meal for my next date, won't you?" I cock my head curiously to one side. "Although you might be a little much to eat. There sure is a lot of you. Wouldn't want to get gluttonous now, would I? Ooh no, now *that* would be terrible..."

# Sloth

I hate my job.

    Now, I know everyone says that, but I *really* hate it. It's such an effort. *Such* an effort. All to make sure stress is the biggest killer of humans.

    Silly really. I'm not needed anymore. Humans are capable of stressing themselves out, thank you very much. With their jobs, their anxiety, their need for perfection in an imperfect world. They do a fantastic job of making their own lives complicated.

    Stupid. But means I'm not needed. Not any longer.

    Yet *He* makes me continue. It's never enough for *Him*. *He* clicks his fingers and I've got to do what I'm told.

    Must be nice to be *Him*.

    I want command, but I don't have the energy to get it. That's what *He* wants, for *His* workers to be unable to fight him off.

    "Come on, Night Hag." I hate that nickname, but everyone refers to me as that whether I want it or not, so I may as well accept it. "Let's go and ruin some lives. Cause some more stress. Can't be lazy, *He* will find out."

    It isn't hard to be me, I suppose. Lying on top of sleeping humans and ensuring they can't move, all while projecting their worst nightmares come to life in front of them...it could be worse.

    But still, I hate it.

    Still, it's too much for me.

    I bring their nightmares into the real world, give them sleep paralysis as the humans call it, and then leave them to go about their day, shrouded in stress. A ticking time bomb, ready to die at any given moment, willing to hand their souls over without thought.

Anxiety too, that can be fun, but the effort is too much for me. I'd rather just do nothing. Save myself the hassle.

"Who is it today? Ah, a gentleman. Finn Smith. Well, Finn, I don't know what you've done to upset *Him*, but it seems like I'm coming for you. I hope you're ready."

It's never the bad guys, the ones who deserve it, because of course, *He* likes them. Plus, stress doesn't normally affect them so much.

No, it's the nice people who've experienced something bad. It's more punishment for them. I make them see it again and again, all while paralyzing them until they are at the tip of their pressure cooker and ready to erupt.

I hope Finn doesn't have a weak heart, I don't like it when they croak out with me in the room. Makes me feel responsible for something I never really wanted.

Plus, it makes my day so much longer.

I find myself in Finn's bedroom in the blink of an eye. He's spread-eagled on the bed sheets, the heat forcing him to sleep naked, not a sight I need. I'm going to get Finn out the way quickly so I don't have to spend any more time with him than absolutely necessary.

"Right, Finn." I rub my hands together. "What do you got for me then? Let's take a look inside your mind to find the horrors of your past."

I don't find much, not at first. This seems to be a man who lives without horror. Hmm, I'm not used to this, I don't know what I'll work with. Why has *He* sent me here...?

"Oh shit!"

I leap back as the first image flashes in front of me. Now *this* is different. This isn't just a man who's lived through horrors, he creates them.

"A killer? A serial killer? But...that makes no sense. I don't understand. Doesn't *He* like that?"

Something isn't right here, something feels all kinds of wrong, but I can't put my finger on it. I'm alert now, more alert than ever and I don't like it one bit.

"This is the wrong house." I'm cold, ice-cold, I feel sick. "I need to get out of here."

But running against the wall doesn't help me escape, trying to get through the door does nothing either. *He* has me trapped here because this must be the guy. Unfortunately, I'm going to have to learn more about this sick fuck to work with him.

"Okay, Finn." I cock my head to each side. "I guess we're going to have to find a way to make this work."

I don't want to touch him again, the idea hurts me, but I do. The images shoot painfully through my body, they ache and crush me, this man is the worst.

He's killed. He's tortured. He's done terrible things to everyone. Men, women, children, there doesn't seem to be a pattern, he doesn't care who he hurts. How can that be?

I might not know much about serial killers, but this doesn't seem right. This feels too much.

I can't breathe.

Oh my God, I can't breathe.

"S...stop this," I rasp to no one. "Stop, I can't take it anymore. Who *is* this?"

Finn has me pinned down now, I don't even know how that's happened, but he's on top of me, fixing me in place, making me unable to move while all my worst nightmares come true around me. He's punishing me by killing me over and over again while I can't do a damn thing to stop it.

I didn't want this job, I didn't want any of this, why the hell am I being punished?

"That's why," Finn hisses over me, spittle flying over my frozen face. "You have to put your whole self into it, you lazy slob, Night Hag. You gave *Him* nothing and now *He* has given you to me. You're my brand new toy because I've given *Him* so many souls, and I have decades of plans with what to do with you. Just know that you're laziness will now become you. You can no longer move ever again, you'll live under endless stress for the rest of your pathetic existence. Or mine, I'm sure you'll be on this plane for longer than me. Then you'll be onto the next lucky asshole."

*No,* I want to cry out, but now my mouth has sealed shut as well. *No, no, no.*

But there's nothing I can do, no one's coming to save me, I'm a demon stuck in the hands of a serial killer. There's no bigger stress than this.

I won't survive it, yet I won't have any choice, and all because I'm a little lazy and I hate my job...

# Envy

I want what I can't have, what I don't have, what someone else has. That's always been my problem.

I don't ever see it as a problem though, because I don't sit around and do nothing about it. I'm not one of those who moans all their life. I take action. I do something about it.

And right now, I want what *she* has.

Mrs. Jones has it all. The gorgeous husband, all the money, the big house, the cute kids, the kick-ass career...

She has it, and I want it, so I will get it. Sure, it might get messy on the way, but it'll be worth it, it always is.

"Hey there, Elizabeth." I grin like we're the best of friends. It's always better to keep my subjects close. Actually, I *have* to have them close to me, connected, bonded somehow, or I can't consumed them. "How are things with you today? You look gorgeous as always. Hardly a surprise, you've looked nice since I moved in last month..."

She titters with laughter and I join in. I make it sound real.

"Oh, aren't you so sweet, Gwen. I feel a mess. So harassed. Today has been *such* a difficult one for me..."

She has nothing to complain about, *nothing*, but she finds a way. Probably so I don't feel bad for not being her.

Yet.

If only she knew...

"Oh, well if you ever want to come around for a coffee and a natter, I'm always here. I'm good with an open ear."

Her face flickers with delight. "Oh, you know I might take you up on that some time. It'd be nice to get to know you a little better, and I do love an open ear. How about wine? You got that too?"

I nod. "Always a bottle chilling in the fridge."

"Perfect. Well, as soon as I get a moment, we can hang out."

And then the real fun will begin.

"AH, ELIZABETH JONES, please come in." I smile brightly and invite her inside my home. Well, I say *my* home, that isn't strictly true. "It's good to have you here at last. I bet you have had a busy week."

"Oh, like you wouldn't believe! Work has been such a stress and the family...well, you know what they're like..."

She trails off awkwardly when she realizes that of course I, Gwen, doesn't know what a family is like because I don't have one.

"Oh, I'm sure." I need to ease the tension, I don't want her to feel awkward. "I can't even begin to imagine, but I bet it's rewarding too. You have all those people relying on you and loving you. It must be nice."

Elizabeth knows she can't complain anymore, not without looking like a real bitch, so she doesn't.

"Tell me about your week," she says instead. "I would love to know more about you, Gwen."

"Oh, not much to tell really." I pour us both a generous glass of wine. "Work has been quiet, but that's what I wanted...a quiet life. It's why I got the job at the library. A place which isn't used so much these days. Not with the Internet."

"Oh, don't get me started on the bloody Internet..."

And with that, any awkwardness is gone, we share a common hate which we can both laugh about...

WAKING UP IN A NEW bed is *always* a nice feeling. Waking up as Elizabeth Jones is something else. I always knew her husband was hot, but *wow*, that body is something else. He is fit!

Of course, Elizabeth in Gwen's body, will soon be here to ruin it, to kick off at me, but I can soon shut her up. She's got to live as boring Gwen now, who lives in too much peace.

I thought I'd like that. Turns out I didn't.

But *this* I do like, this I like a whole lot.

"Hey there, handsome." I shake him and wake him up. "How are you this morning? You look good!"

I'm hoping that me and him can get a little freaky. My life as Gwen left me...well barren. It's one of the hazards of shape-shifting, but I know I hit the jackpot this time. I might not even need to shift again.

"What the fuck did you wake me up for?"

*Oh!* I wasn't expecting that at all. I thought this was a nice man, not someone who would speak to his beautiful wife like that.

"Sorry, I just thought it could be fun..."

I feel deflated. Flat like a balloon going down. Last night, switching bodies, made me so thrilled. I just *knew* this would be the right decision, but now...

*No*, I warn myself. *No, give this life a chance.*

I've shifted to so many people, I've had so many disappointments, it's hard not to judge quickly. But I need an open mind. I wanted Elizabeth and that's what I've got.

"Well, I had a late night last night with the kids while you were out until some ridiculous hour so I don't want to hear it."

"Ten PM is a ridiculous hour?" I'm stunned. "Really?"

"Just fuck off, Liz. Let me sleep."

With a new weight on my shoulder, I head downstairs for breakfast and to meet my kids properly for the first time. Then I'll have my job, surely that'll make up for my husband's attitude. By the end of the day, I'll be overjoyed and all of this will be forgotten...

"GWEN." I HAMMER ON her door hard. Turns out I'm the one coming to her not the other way around. This never happens, but I've never experience a life like this before. "Gwen, open up."

"Oh, hi, *Elizabeth*." I roll my eyes at her unnecessary mocking tone. "Do come in again."

I follow her inside the home I already miss. Gwen's life wasn't all that bad, why did I have to think the grass would be greener somewhere else? If only I could go back, but shape shifters can't return once they leave a body.

"What is with your life?" I demand as soon as we're safely locked inside and no one can hear us.

"Oh, you mean the abusive husband, the God-awful job where they walk all over me, and the ungrateful kids? Yeah, you're welcome to that."

She sucks in a pointed deep breath and turns to face me with an easy smile. One I've never seen her wear before and not just because it's a new mouth she has.

"I've always been jealous of Gwen, you know. Her easy, quiet life. I've always wanted it for myself." She chuckles as if this whole situation amuses her. "I noticed her changing a little after she made friends with a new woman from work."

"Alice." That's who I was before. Her life was a nightmare as well.

"Right, Alice, and then she became *you*, right?" I nod, surprised at how much she knows. "Then all of a sudden, Gwen wanted to be close to me. My husband called it desperate and tried to stop it happening, but I insisted. I just had this *feeling* that befriending Gwen would work in my favor and give me my freedom somehow. I didn't know how exactly, but I knew it would be good. I've always been intuitive like that."

"So, you knew *something*? Yet you didn't stop me?"

"Hey, if you wanted my life, then you are welcome to it. It's shit, truly awful. And now I get to live as Gwen which is what I have always wanted."

I'm so stunned that it takes me a few moments to speak. The grass was greener, but not for me, for Elizabeth. I thought her life was perfect.

"Good luck befriending anyone else to escape that hell, by the way," she chuckles boldly. "My husband doesn't let me have friends. He nearly killed me because I wanted to hang out with you. Have you had your beating for it yet?" I shake my head, shocked into silence. "Oh, well it's coming, so you better prepare for it."

"Oh no." I feel sick. I might throw up. "What have I done? What am I going to do?"

"Not my problem anymore. All I can say to you is be careful what you wish for because it might just come true."

I'm stuck in this mess, at least for the foreseeable future, which means I'm about to live the worst nightmare ever, and all because I always want what I can't have, what I *shouldn't* have...

# Greed

T he dead don't talk.

That's what they always say.

The dead *can't* talk.

That's a theory of the living, but *we* know better. Not only can the dead talk, they always have a lot to say, but none as much as me. I have tons to say and nothing will get in my way.

I'm finding a way to say it all, no matter what it takes.

He hasn't heard the last of me, and the next words he hears from me will be his last.

Another thing they always say is 'revenge is a dish best served cold'. I don't know how true that is but I'm about to find out.

Watching him work on his latest project like he's some kinda genius enrages me. Not only can the dead feel the same emotions as the living, the way we feel them is intensified by about a million times. Anger isn't just anger anymore. It's full-blown, all-consuming rage.

Right now, all of that is directed at him.

Does he feel it?

He touches the prickles I want to project on the back of his neck. He shudders, shivers, but it isn't enough. It's never enough. Yet. But it will be.

"Oh, Landon, you have no idea what's coming for you, do you? You thought you saw the last of me when you left me alone in that dodgy Mexican motel. Well, you might've choked the life from me, left me black and blue, but I'm back and ready for action. But how to torment you best."

Landon is a materialistic man, one who adores his possessions. Seems silly to me, I wasn't ever like that in life, but if it's the way to crush him, then that's how I shall do it.

"You think you can swan through life, acting like you want to and nothing will happen, just because you got money? Well, that's before you strangled Kristin Matthews."

A growl erupts from me. I was just a foolish girl, swept away by the romance this man could offer me. I thought he was amazing and I couldn't believe someone like him would even *look* at me...but of course, that's what he wanted me to think.

I was just the latest young girl, the newest fool, the flavor of the week, and Landon knew I was always going to end up left for dead somewhere because that's what he does.

He was born into money, he's never had to aim for anything, work for a damn thing, life has just been handed to him on a plate, which meant he needed to get his thrills another way.

And he sure found his kink.

I now know that his first kill was at thirteen-years-old. A maid who worked in his house, a beautiful woman in her early twenties, who fell for him like I did.

She had no idea their sordid love affair would result in her death, just like I didn't.

His father helped him then, got rid of the body for him, and basically taught Landon that with enough money at his disposal he can do anything, bribe anyone, get away with whatever.

His father raised an entitled little shit and I'm going to be the one to take him down. Other ghosts might have more right to destroy him, but they haven't, so I guess it's up to me.

"You are fucked, Landon, and you are about to find out just how much..."

THEFT IS FUN. IT'S not something I ever would've been a part of when I was alive, but that's because I led a good life...not that it led me anywhere positive. But dead, I can do what I want and I'm enjoying it more than I thought I would.

"Oh no, where are your keys, Landon?"

God I love teasing him, I just wish he could hear me. It would be so much better if he could hear me.

"Oh no, what happened to your cell phone, Landon? What a shame. It must be really hard for you..."

Seeing him lose his mind over his shit is funny, but I don't know if it's enough. I thought it might be enough but I'm not satisfied enough.

He killed me, I need to do more than just toy with him.

"What can I do to him? What can I do to this murdering fuck to make him see what an idiot he is? Greed is his lifestyle, but greed isn't taking him down enough. I need more."

He's at his computer, on his email, messaging a woman. That's how it often starts with him, or so I've learned. This is part of his so-called charm.

The emails are part of the foreplay for him, the foray into murder. I need to do something quick or another woman will cross over to the other side like me.

I want to be his last.

I want to touch him, to hurt him first, but I can't. That isn't in the rules. So, what the hell can I do?

Who are the emails for? What's the woman's name? Maybe I can get to her first, talk to her in the way only the dead can, make her see that she needs to kill him before he kills her.

*Ana Thomas.*

I need to locate her...

"You think I can't see you, Kristen?" His voice chills me. I didn't know it was possible to get any colder. "You think I don't hear you and your little snippy comments? Honestly, I thought more of you than that."

He stares at me dead in the eyes. He really can see me.

"This is why you're dead. Why all of you are dead." As Landon makes a sweeping gesture with his hands, more spirits appear in my vision. All of them dead-eyed and miserable. "To keep you with me forever. Once I claim a woman, she's always mine. *Always*. Even the afterlife won't get in our way. Now, I let you fuck around with me for a bit because I know how you all want revenge, but let's be honest, none of you had any real life anyway. You aren't much of a loss to the world." But the games stop now, Kristen, because I'm about to bring Ana into my little army as well. She's hot and fiery, a bit like you, so once I kill her you may even get along. Now come on, we're going now."

There's a magnetic pull. I don't want to follow him but it seems like I have no choice. None of us do. We have to go with him while he murders Ana and there isn't a damn thing we can do about it.

No wonder everyone else is dead-eyed.

Landon isn't only an entitled little shit, he also owns all of us. He killed us and now we belong to him for the rest of his life, and maybe even after that.

Where the fuck is the justice in that?

# Samie Sands

S amie Sands is the author of the AM13 Outbreak series—Lockdown, Forgotten, Extinct, and Not Dead Yet. She's also had a number of short stories published in very successful short story anthologies. To find out more about her and her work, check out her website at **http://samiesands.com.**

**Facebook.com/SamieSandsLockdown**[1]
**Twitter.com/SamieSands**[2]
**Wattpad.com/SamieSands**[3]
**Amazon.com/SamieSands**[4]

---

1.    https://www.Facebook.com/SamieSandsLockdown/

2.    https://twitter.com/SamieSands

3.    https://www.wattpad.com/user/SamieSands

4.    https://www.amazon.com/Samie-Sands/e/B00JWQJS4C/
      ref=sr_ntt_srch_lnk_1?qid=1549532732&sr=8-1

# Ice Man
## Steve Thorne

The Devil walked away as Johnny bent to retrieve his prize. It felt heavy, being made of solid gold, but as he drew the bow across the golden strings, it felt as comfortable as his own wooden fiddle, and the sound it made was incredible. How could he have beaten the Devil against this instrument? The sound is fantastic, and it plays like finest Stradivarius. Obviously his skill is far greater than he had believed, and with this golden fiddle, he would be the best fiddle player in the world.

Johnny played more jigs on his new fiddle. Ol' Joe Clark, Orang Blossom Special, Jamestown Ferry, and many others that he had only heard, but never played before. Everything came out perfect. All he had to do was think of a tune, and he could play it like it was ingrained into his repertoire. Johnny put his new golden fiddle into his case and left the woods.

Johnny climbed the rickety wooden steps to his second floor apartment, carrying the case with his golden fiddle. He burst through the door, shouting, "Louella!", and Louella came running from the bathroom, her jeans hugged her hips and her plaid cotton shirt was buttoned part way, then tied in a knot at her midriff, and her hair was wrapped in a kerchief as ran into the living room carrying a washcloth and a bottle of disinfectant.

"What is it Johnny!" she said, concern running across her face, "What's wrong baby?"

"Nothing's wrong sugah," he said, "In fact, everything is gonna be alright from now on."

"Whatchoo on about baby?" Louella said as she put her cleaning supplies down.

"This!" Johnny said, as he lifted his fiddle case up and showed it to her."

"Baby, we done talked about this. You are good, baby, real good, but there are too many fiddlers out there. You ain't gonna make it. You need money, you need agents, you need contacts. Baby, it is too big a risk. You ain't gonna be a professional fiddler baby."

"You don't get it sugah." Johnny said as he placed the case on the table, "This is a special fiddle. This here's the Devil's fiddle."

"What're you on abouts baby?" Louella said.

"I was in the woods, fiddling, like I do on Saturday's, when the Devil came to me and bet me I couldn't best him at fiddle playin'."

"You been drinkin' again baby?"

"No Louella, it was real. He was there. The Devil hisself, bettin' he could beat me, ME, of all people, at fiddlin'"

"The Devil?" Louella said, her hands on her hips, "All red, with horns and a tail and all?"

"No, he was wearin' a seersucker suit, and bowtie."

"Johnny, you ain't making sense baby. The devil don't walk around in a seersucker suit looking like Colonel Saunders baby, and he ain't gonna bet you in fiddle playin' contest. That's absurd."

"It's true sugah," Johnny pleaded, "Just hear me out. Don't believe me if'n you don't wanna, but listen, then I will prove it to you."

"O.K." Louella said, "Tell me the story how you bested Ol' Scratch in a fiddle contest."

"Like I said," Johnny started again, "I was playing my fiddle, and playing it hot, when the Devil jumps on a hickory stump and says Boy, lemme tell ya what."

"Did the Devil happen to look like Charlie Daniel?" Louella asked, shaking her head.

"OK, you ain't gonna listen to the story, then let me show you." and with that Johnny opened up the case and took out his shiny gold fiddle. Louella's mouth dropped open as she stared at the gleaming fiddle.

"Is that... is ..."

"Yeah, It is." Johnny said, "A fiddle made o' gold. Beat Ol' Scratch fair'n square."

"You have any idea how much this is worth?" Louella said, as she reached for it.

Johnny pulled the fiddle away fast, and slapped her hand away from it.

"NO!" he shouted, "It's mine. I won it, it's mine."

Louella was taken aback by the sudden violence, but held her hands up in defeat, then said, "But baby, you can't play a metal fiddle, it ain't gonna sound good at all."

"You think?" Johnny said, and a smile played across his face. "Name me a song, any song."

"Play The Legend of Wooley Swamp." Louella asked.

"It wasn't Charlie Daniels, it was the Devil!" Johnny shouted at her.

"Just play the song baby." She said, smirking at him. Johnny started to play the song on his golden fiddle, and it flowed out of him like he had been playing it all his life. Louella started dancing to it, and getting caught up in the story of the ghost of Lucius Clay, when Johnny finished the song, Louella clapped for him. "That was wonderful Johnny." she said, "I have never heard you play like that before. That was amazing."

"I tell ya sugah, I can play anything. Any song I ever heard, any song I have ever played, better'n I ever had."

"Do Garth Brooks." she said, "I like me some To Make You Feel My Love."

"For you sugah, anything." and as Johnny started to play, he thought about the sentiment of the song, the love, the emotion, as he played the song."

Louella started to dance again the the music coming from the golden fiddle. She was swaying her hips, eyes closed, just getting lost in the music. She pulled open the knot at her waist, and let shirt hang at her side as she started to undo the buttons going up her front when Johnny stopped.

"Louella, what are you doing?"

Louella stopped her dancing and realized she had started to undo her shirt.

"It's that Devil Fiddle doin' that!" she yelled, backing away from Johnny and his possessed instrument.

"So now you believe it's the Devil's Fiddle?"

"Get rid of it Johnny. Get rid of that evil thing." then she looked around and said, "Where's your fiddle Johnny, the one I gave you for our anniversary."

Johnny looked around, as if just now realizing he did not have the fiddle he used to beat the Devil. "I, I don't know. I guess I left it in the woods."

"In the woods?" she said, tension in her voice, "The fiddle I bought you, you just LEFT IT, in the woods?"

"Sugah, this is so much better. I don't need that old thing anymore."

"You don't need that, that, that old thing, anymore? Is that what you think, that you just discard, old things you don't need anymore?"

"Sugah, I didn't mean ..."

"Didn't mean what? Didn't mean to throw a treasured memory away for a shiny new toy?"

"I'll, I'll get it sugah, I will, I promise." Johnny stammered.

Louella buttoned her shirt again, and picked up the case for the fiddle.

"Get out. Take that evil thing out of here, and you bring back your original fiddle." and she pushed the case to him, and started to push him out the door. "Don't come back with, with, with THAT thing, and you had better have YOUR fiddle with you." and as he crossed the threshold, she slammed the door behind him.

Johnny made his way back to the spot where he confronted the Devil, but could not find his fiddle anywhere. He looked all over, under logs, behind rocks, nothing. He sat on the same stump the Devil sat upon earlier, and sighed. What was he going to do? Louella made it clear, he had to have the fiddle, or he wasn't getting back into the apartment without it.

"Well, nothing I can for now. Maybe if I get some flowers, or some take-out. She has been working all day, maybe a treat will smooth things over." and with that thought, he stood and headed back into town. As he walked to the florist, he noticed a fiddle in the pawn shop. Not exactly his, but maybe it was close enough. He stopped in the store to inquire about the fiddle.

"She's a beaut," the man said, "Sounds great. I'm willing to part with it for say, two-fifty?"

"Two hundred and fifty dollars?" Johnny said.

"Sure'nuff." the man said, "Quality instrument like that, probably a good grand new."

Johnny knew he did not have that much money on him and he knew he did not have that much in the bank, even if he could get it without Louella finding out. What to do, what to do.

"When do you close?" he asked the man.

"Nine tonight, why? Gotta ask permission?" he smirked.

"Something like that." Johnny said, "Don't sell it tonight, I will be back."

"You look like a good guy, tell ya what, come back tonight, with cash, I can let it go for two."

"Got yourself a deal mister." Johnny said, "I will be back tonight, just don't sell it, and I will have the money." and Johnny left, wondering how he was going to get the money.

The weight of the solid gold fiddle was wearing on him. When he played it, it was as light as any fiddle he ever had, but now, it was starting to bear down on him. Johnny leaned against a lamp post and put his golden fiddle down, and opened the case. He started to rosin the hairs of the bow, which were made of fine spun golden thread, same as the bow, the fiddle, and the strings on the fiddle. The entirety of the instrument was solid gold, but it sounded incredible nonetheless.

He started to play the fiddle, starting with some bluegrass, a little creole, and some good old country tunes. Soon, there was a crowd gathered around, and they were throwing money into his open case. The crowd was getting bigger, and it was a party on the street. Johnny spied an attractive red head watching, and clapping, and dancing, but he had not seen her put anything into the case.

As he continued playing, he interacted with the audience, playing the occasional request, when he looked at the woman and casual said. "Like the music?"

She smiled at him and nodded, still dancing.

"How about you show me some appreciation." he said, and she just shrugged her shoulder and mouthed, "No money"

"Throw in your top, we call it even." he joked, grinning at her, but then, she pulled her top off and threw it into the case. Johnny stopped, and everyone just stared at her, when she realized what she had done, she grabbed her shirt, and ran away. Johnny shrugged, started playing again, and the party continued.

Soon the crowd started to thin out, along with the hopes that the red head would return, and Johnny thanked everyone for their patronage and counted his cash. He had made over $500 in the hour he was playing and thought this was the best. He made it to the pawn shop by eight-thirty.

"Still have it, like you asked." the man said as he pulled the fiddle from its display, "Two Hundred, like I promised, if you have the cash."

Johnny looked at him and a thought entered his mind. First Louella, then the red head, got him wondering. "I am going to need a case for the fiddle, do you have one?"

"What's wrong with the one you have there?" he said, pointing to the case at Johnny's feet.

"Oh, this one?" he smirked, "This one is full." and with that, he opened the case and pulled out his golden fiddle.

"Why are you buying this old thing when you have that?" he asked.

Johnny took out his golden fiddle and started to play for the man. He ran the bow across the strings a few times, and it made an evil hiss, then he went into Turkey in the Straw, and the man was clapping with the song. While he was still playing, Johnny asked, "So, what do you say, for such a fine impromptu show, you give me the fiddle, and the case?" but Johnny kept playing as he awaited the man's answer.

"For a fiddle player of your caliber, young man, that is a deal I will take any time." and he put the fiddle in the case and left it on the counter for Johnny. Johnny finished his set, put away his golden fiddle, and took both and left as quickly as possible. He suspected the enchantment might not last long, and he did not want to be around when the man came to his senses.

Once he was far enough away, Johnny ducked into an alley, and put the wooden fiddle in his old fiddle case, and his golden fiddle into the new case, pulled up a milk carton, sat down, and pondered how he was going to get his golden fiddle into the apartment without Louella knowing he still had it.

"Fuck it." he said to himself. "It is my home too. If I want the best fiddle I have ever played, and use it to make a name for myself, I am going to do it." and with that thought in his mind, he grabbed both cases, and headed back home. Johnny opened the door quietly. He was not sure what kind of mood Louella was going to be in, but he opened the door anyway, and walked in.

"Lou ..." Johnny started when suddenly Louella was in his arms kissing him.

"Johnny, baby, I am sorry. I was so worried. You have been gone so long, are you alright?"

Johnny hugged her as she kissed him, then slowly let her go as she lowered herself back to her feet.

"I'm OK sugah." he said, and I am sorry I was late but look," and he fanned out the bills in front of her, and her eyes lit up."

"Johnny," she said, "What have you been doing? You been gambling again"

"No Louella," he said as he dropped the bills on the table, "I was fiddlin'. I was fiddlin' on the street corner and people done gimme money. I was buskin', not gamblin'"

"With, with, with that Devil Fiddle?" she asked noticing the two cases.

Johnny pulled out his golden fiddle and said, "Yes Louella, with this. This is the finest instrument ever."

"But it is evil, Johnny." Louella explained. "Noting good can possibly come of it. You found your old fiddle, why can't you busk with that one instead?"

"Mario Andretti can probably race in any car, but the better the driver, the better the car he deserves. It just compliments his natural talent, that is what my golden fiddle does for me baby. It makes me better."

"If you need the fiddle to be good, are you really all that good?"

"My golden fiddle does not make me good, it makes me better." Johnny said, as he pulled his golden fiddle out of the case, "Listen sugah," he said as he started to play the fiddle. He thought about the song he played, and how it should sound, and how Louella will love it, and accept it, and agree that it is his talent being accentuated by the incredible tone of the fiddle, and as he played, Louella swayed to the music, hugging herself, smiling as she was totally caught up in the music.

When he finally stopped playing, Louella was still mesmerized by his music, just swaying to the memory in her head of the music.

"Did you like that sugah?" he asked, and as if she was in a dream Louella just smiled at him and softly cooed, "Nothing that sound like that can be evil."

Before Johnny put his golden fiddle away, he played one more tune, and as Louella was completely taken by the tune, he said, "This is a good thing, sugah, and never forget it." He then put his golden fiddle in its case, and took Louella in his arms and kissed her. "It's been a long day sugah, let's go to bed."

Johnny and Louella stayed a little longer in bed Sunday morning, having enjoyed a passionate night, and as the sun shone through their curtains, they slowly aroused. Louella looked at the clock, and sat up.

"Johnny, we are gonna be late for church!" she said

"Relax sugah," Johnny said, "We can catch the 11:00 service, then I thought I could go out and busk a bit."

"Can you busk on a Sunday?" Louella asked.

"No laws I know about it. Only where, not so much when. 'sides, I know a few gospel tunes that will grace my collection plate. Are you alright with that?"

Louella was worried for a moment, but could not remember why. All she could say was, "It's a good thing baby." then they dressed in their Sunday best, and went to church.

After the service, Louella said she was going home to make dinner for him.

"When y'all gonna be back baby?" she asked.

"it's one now, whatya say we get some lunch, spread some of the wealth around, then I'll busk for a coupla three hours, if the people don't mind, then should be home for dinner." then pulling out some more bills, he gave Louella a hundred dollars, and said, "Get us a ham for dinner, and a bottle of wine. We'll have a right proper dinner."

Louella looked at the money in her hand and back at Johnny.

"Are you sure baby? We have other needs, other bills. This could go a long way baby."

"Don't you worry dear. I'll bring home three times that tonight, just you watch, now go, make us a nice dinner, and do something nice for yourself, I'll see you soon." and he patted her bottom as she walked toward the butcher.

Johnny walked the streets until he found what he hoped was a good spot. Lots of people out for a Sunday stroll. Johnny opened his case and took out his golden fiddle, and drew the bow across the strings, and it made that same eerie hissing sound as before, but as he started into 'In the Sweet By and By', people stopped and listened. A crowd was forming and people started to put money in his case. When he went into Foggy Mountain Breakdown, some people started to dance, and more people threw in money and soon it was like a Baptist Revival, with people singing and dancing and clapping and making donations and everyone was having a wonderful time. One man was standing away from the crowd, leaning against a lamp post, and watched the festivities with a keen interest, when a movement caught his eye, and he noticed a cop coming down the street. No one else seemed to, but the man moved a little out of the way so it would not look so much like he was part of the crowd when the cop pushed through and moved toward Johnny, who had not stopped playing.

"I am going to have to ask you to leave sir." the cop said, very politely, but very authoritative, "You are creating a disturbance, and I will this party to disband." then turning to the crowd, he yelled over the din, "Please everyone, I need you to leave the area. You are creating a disturbance, please exit the area immediately."

Johnny continued playing, this time a fiery tune that got peoples blood pumping and he shouted over the crowd, "Do you want me to stop people?"

"NO!" came the group in unison.

"This man wants us to stop the Lords work. He wants us to forget our heritage, he wants us to conform. Do you want that?"

"NO!" the people shouted again.

"Please, everyone," the cop shouted, "I am asking you kindly, please, disperse from this area."

"NO!" the crowd shouted.

"What are you going to do about it, my congregation!" Johnny shouted, and the crowd started to move in on the police office.

The office blew his whistle to get their attention, but the people started to push him. The cop pulled his walky-talky and tried to call for help when one of the people grabbed it from his hand and hit him with it. The crowd became frenzied, and people where kicking and punching the cop. They used canes if they had them, or fists. Someone found a rock and threw it at the police officer.

Seeing the direction the crowd was going, Johnny quickly closed his case and took his fiddle and ran away as the stranger watched him leave, before he too, moved away from the frenzied crowd.

Johnny reached his apartment, winded, but excited at the experience.

"You're home early baby, how was the busking?"

Johnny just leaned against the door, trying to catch his breath.

"You alright baby?" Louella asked as she came into the living room to see Johnny breathing heavy against the door. "What's wrong?"

Johnny put his golden fiddle on the table and opened his case and poured out all the money he had made. Louella just gasped as she sank to her knees and started to pick up the bills, and the coins that were spread all over the floor. Johnny joined her on the floor, and started to gather the money into like piles, as Johnny told her about the events on the street.

"It was so strange sugah," he said, "I was just playing good old gospel music, and the people were gathering and throwing money, and, whoa!" Johnny said as he held up a hundred dollar bill, "Ain't ever seen one a these up close, have you?" and as Luella took the bill, and smiled, Johnny continued with his story.

"Anyways, I am playing and the crowd is dancing and clapping and laughing when this cop shows up to tell us to leave, and then the crowd is all hell no, we won't go, and he starts barking orders and the people is all getting uppity about him stopping the concert and the starts getting mean and pushing and hitting, and throwing things and..."

"Oh my god Johnny, are you alright?" Louella interrupted.

"No, yes, yes I am alright, I just closed my case and headed away from there as fast as possible.

"One Thousand, three hundred and eighty-six dollars and, thirty, forty, forty-five and one two three, eight, forty eight cents." Louella finished counting, "Who the hell puts pennies in the kitty? I am glad you are safe. I did not know the people could be so violent, and onna Sunday ta boot."

"Less not think on it anymore sugah, less just put this money away fer now, have ourselves that nice ham dinner you been cookin' and enjoy our good luck." Johnny said.

After dinner the two did the dishes, and sat down on the sofa to watch the news. The lead story was about the riot downtown. It was scary, but apparently the news crew showed up after Johnny had left. The only clue to his involvement was stunned, and embarrassed people, just mentioning they were listening to a fiddle player, but no one could identify him by name, or even describe him, all they knew was he had a gold fiddle. They could not even explain why they attacked the policeman, just that they were enjoying themselves, when the officer tried to stop them, and they suddenly felt a vindictive anger to the man, but then suddenly the feeling was gone and the office was laying on the ground and other policemen were there and the whole things was confusing and scary.

"Oh Johnny," Louella said as she got up to turn the TV off, "I am glad you got out of there when you did, maybe then woulda turned on you too." when suddenly there was a knock on the door. "Hide fiddle baby." she said, not really sure why, but just feeling wary as she walked to the door. Louella opened the door, but did not take the chain off and asked, "Yes?"

"Well hello miss...?" and he paused for Louella to supply her name. After a few moments, when she did not say anything he continued, "Anyway, I am looking for a young man named Johnny, does he happen to be here at the moment?"

"What is this in regards to?" Louella asked.

Sensing the woman behind the door was trying to protect her friend, he said, "I am a talent agent. I heard him in the park today, and I would like to represent him. So, is he here?"

Johnny just came into the room from hiding his golden fiddle and nodded his head vigorously, waving Louella to let him in.

"What if he's a cop, coming to arrest you?" she whispered to Johnny.

"I am not a cop, and I have not desire to arrest the best fiddle player I have ever heard. Here is my card." he said, passing his card through the door. It was a glossy black card with shiny red lettering that said ...

JOSHUA CAMPBELL

Talent Scout

Memphis Tennessee

"Looks legit." Louella said, then turning back to the man at the door, "Just a minnit." and she closed the door, undid the chain, and opened the door, looking out to the street as she let the man in before closing and chaining the door again.

The man walked into the room, and Johnny came to meet him, hand extended as Louella sat back onto the sofa, and offered the man the chair. Johnny joined her on the sofa, across from Joshua.

"So, that was rather intense at the park today, wasn't it?" Joshua said, then holding his hands up to stop the protest he could see forming on Johnny's face, "I do not think you were responsible for the crowd

Johnny." he said, "I am not here for any reason than to sign you as a client. If anyone was to attribute what happened today to you, it s only because your music moved them. You are amazing, and I am sure I can make you a star."

"And what's in it for you?" Louella asked, "Why you wanna rep my man?"

"Smart woman you got there Johnny, I like her." then turning to look at both Johnny and Louella, "I book all your gigs. Everything goes through me, shows, appearances, articles, get vetted by me, and for that, I take 20% of the booking fee."

"Don't most agents take only 10%" Louella asked.

"Some do, I don't. To be honest, I will work my ass off for your man. I will have playing the Opry inside a year, and to be frank, I charge what I charge cuz I am the st that's ever been at this."

Louella was still wary of this man, but Johnny was all smiles once he hears 'the Opry inside a year'.

"Mr. Campbell," Johnny said, as he held out his hand, just as Louella jabbed his ribs, then taking Joshua's hand in his, said, "Thank you for coming. I wanna talk this over with my wife, may I call you tomorrow? after work?"

"Number's on the card. Don't be waiting too long, but I hope to hear from you tomorrow." and with that, he stood and walkd to the door. Louella let him out, chained and bolted the door.

"I told ya sugah." Johnny said, "I told you, things were looking up. I told you that my golden fiddle would make our dreams come true. You get that, right? This is good right?"

Louella looked at Johnny, smiled, and said, "It's alright baby."

Johnny and Louella talked about Josh's offer for an hour or so, but it was late and they both had to go to work in the morning. The next day, Johnny was so excited at work. He was telling everyone e was discovered by big talent scout and he was sure he was going to be famous soon. That night, when he gt home, he told Louella that he thought they should take the deal.

"What about your job?" she asked, "You have seniority. You have a pension and healthcare. What about that?"

"I talked it over with Mike, he is alright with me fiddling on the side, as long as I make my shift in the morning. Actually wished me the best. Seems he always wanted to play guitar in a band but never had the guts. Even told me to tell him when and where I'll be playing my first gig Says he wants to be able to say he knew me when."

"Make the call baby, but you make sure this thing don't skew up what you got going right now."

"I won't sugah. 'sides I got you to keep me on the straight and narrow We are a team. You are the angel on my shoulder, making sure I am doing the right thing." and as Johnny called Joshua to tell him he was on board, Louella could not help but think, "But am I strong enough to fight the Devil on your other shoulder?"

Joshua was knocking on their door within the hour, and had the contract with him. The three of them sat at the kitchen table and Joshua went over the contract with hem explaining everything or them, detailing each clause, and allaying any concerns they might have had.

"Are clear on everything?" Joshua asked, "If you have any concerns that I have fully addressed, I implore you to seek out an entertainment lawyer and have him look over the contract. I want both," and he looked at the two of them, swinging his head back and forth to look each of them in the eyes, "of you to be fully committed and positive that this is what you want. Now, do I have to give you two more time?"

"What do you think sugah?" Johnny asked, "You are more smarter than me on these things. Does it look good?"

"Two things I like, one, this will mean a lot of work for you, which is good. It does not look 'too good to be true' cause they never are."

"And the second?" Joshua asked.

"You never once answered my questions with, 'That's just standard.'" Louella said.

"I do like you Louella. You don't take no bull from people, and you talk straight. That is why I don't mind having you around. You look after Johnny, like I am going to do. You care for him, and I think, together, we will take him to the top, but really, like I said, if I have not answered your concerns, you go, tomorrow if you can, get yourself a lawyer to look over the contract, I can wait another day or two, but I need you both to be fully committed to this deal."

"And that is three." she said, "You are practically twisting my arm to get me to have a lawyer look at it. Shows me you ain't hiding anything, or trying to hide anything, but you got here we are responsible for our own transportation, what if you book us outta town, or outta state?"

"That's just standard ..." Joshua started to say when Louella gave him a look, and he finished, "Sorry, but it really is. Even big names, like the Stones, Flatt and Scruggs, hell even Garth Brook pays his own way, well, actually when you get that big, you are considered a corporation, and all the finances like paying to roadies, the transportation companies, even the airlines, are handled by accountants and such, but it still comes outta Garth's pocket, so to speak, but I know Johnny has a job, for now, and I will keep his booking local so he is not doing any overnights, unless they are on a weekend?"

"So Johnny still keeps his job?" Louella said.

"I am hoping soon, this will be his job, but yes, and if you think he can't make the gig, and his job, you let me know, I will work something out. I don't want him losing his job, until he is ready to quit, and you both benefit from the amazing success I know he is going to have."

"Whataya say sugah?" Johnny asked, "You wanna do this, with me?"

"Just so you know, I'm keeping my job. I will support you, I will go to all your shows I am able to, and if this becomes your career, I will be at home waiting when you return, but you are not going to be my sole means of support, and I am not going to be playing tambourine in the band, got that baby?"

"You have always been your own woman Louella, and I love that about you. We can talk about the whole job thing after I make my first million, but for now, you agree to let me sign, and you do you, and I do me, and together we will be an unbeatable team."

Joshua unscrewed the cap off his Montblanc fountain pen and handed it to Johnny, who signed the contract, but as he finished a burr nicked his thumb.

"Ow," Johnny said as a drop of blood fell on the contract, and Joshua took the pen back.

"I am sorry Johnny, are you OK? Do you need a Band-Aide®?" Louella was just coming back in the room with the box of bandages when Johnny pulled his thumb out of his mouth, saying, "Nope. I'm good, see?" and he held his thumb out and the blood had already stopped flowing, "But I smeared your contract, do you need a new one?"

"No, no," Joshua said, "It's alright. It doesn't cover anything, I think the lawyers will be OK with it."

Joshua screwed the cap back on his pen, folded the contract, and said good night to the couple.

"Get a good nights sleep kids, tomorrow, everything changes for you."

Wednesday afternoon, Mike called Johnny in off the floor.

"Hey, Rasmuth, phone!" he shouted, and Johnny came into his office and took the phone.

"Oh hey, hi, yeah, good to hear, so? Yeah, Friday? Seven? Sure I can make it for Seven. I go on at eight, after the first warm up? Great, I will see you then." and as he hung up the phone, Mike looked at him, smiling, and said, "So?"

I gotta gig. I go on at eight, but I gotta be there by seven to be ready. My first real gig."

"Awesome man. Me and Em, will be there with you cheering you on man. That is so incredible. Now, get back to work you lazy bastard." he said as he smiled at Johnny and pushed him out the door.

Friday night could not come fast enough for Johnny. He was practically bouncing off the walls, and when He and Louella showed up at the theatre he was buzzing with excitement. Louella kissed him for luck, then joined Mike and Emily at their table, while Joshua stayed back stage with Johnny. The first act was incredible, and Johnny felt very nervous. All the bravado he felt when he fiddled against the Devil was slowly seeping from him when Joshua took him by the shoulders and looked into his eyes.

"Johnny, listen, you got this." he said, "You need to know that you are the best. Keep that in your mind at all times. This guy." he said, motioning to the man on stage, "is nothing compared to you, you have to keep that in your head at all times while performing. I tried to get you to open, but they did not want anyone untested first, so do not let anything distract you from not believing in yourself. KNOW you are the best, keep that in your heart, and in your mind, and you WILL be the best."

Johnny shook his arms out, feeling the anxiety slowly ebbing from him as the first fiddler finished. He finished, and the crowd erupted in thunderous applause. As the man walked past Johnny, and sidechecked him a little.

"Try to follow that." he said as he left the area.

Johnny started to feel angry, but he could not lose focus. He did what Joshua had said, and pushed all fear and doubt out of his mind, and focused on being the best. They announced Johnny, and his excitement rose. No longer afraid, he felt bolstered as Joshua clapped him on the shoulder, and said, "Knock 'em dead buddy." and he left to join Louella, Mike and Emily at their table.

Johnny came out. He was so small and unassuming, but everyone immediately perked up when they saw his golden fiddle. The crowd hushed. Mesmerized by the shiny instrument, and then Johnny drew his bow across the golden strings and the fiddle made an evil hiss that caused everyone to listen closer at this unknown.

"I would like to dedicate this one to all the women out there. It is a favourite of my wife, Louella, and I hope you like it as well." and Johnny started playing 'To Make You Feel My Love' but instead of focusing on the depth of the song, all he wanted them to feel from his music was how talented he was. He finished the tune, and the crowd applauded, then he went into some jigs and reels, he played some classics, bluegrass, Cajun, even rockabilly, and each tune brought more applause, and each round of applause brought more confidence, and he truly believed he was the best there ever was. When he finished, he bowed his head, and the crowd gave him a standing ovation. Johnny stood there for a moment as the crowd clapped, and whistled, and he lifted his arms, holding his golden fiddle in one hand, and his bow in the other, and soaked up all the applause until he was motioned off stage. As he went back stage, he saw the first fiddle player, and as he passed, Johnny looked him in the eye and said, "THAT, is how you play a fiddle." and left to join his friends at their table.

For the rest of the evening, anyone who passed by Johnny's table had to stop and shake his hand. Ask for his autograph, or take a selfie with him. It was getting to the point that the group could not enjoy the rest of the performers for all the interruptions, but Johnny did not want to seem uncharitable of their affections, but finally the concert was over, and everyone made their way home. Joshua said his goodbye's to the couple, and as he shook Johnny's hand said, "You did good Johnny. Word of this is going to get around. I see many, many more performances to come. Now you go home. Get some sleep. I will be in touch with you as soon as I can, and Louella," he said, looking at her, "Take care of our man here. You two make an excellent couple."

"Thank You Joshua," she said, "I will." and she wrapped her arm around Johnny's waist and held him close before they both left for home.

Monday morning, Johnny walked onto the warehouse floor, and as he made it to the center of the warehouse a voice came across the loudspeaker.

"Ladies and Gentlemen, allow me to introduce to you, the greatest fiddle player EVER!" and everyone in the warehouse clapped for him, some coming up and slapping him on the back. Johnny waited until they gave him some room, and took a bow, thanking them all for their encouragement.

Many more performances were booked, some Mike attended, some he could not, but someone from the plant was always in the audience, and as always, Louella and Joshua were there for him.

One night, after yet another performance, Johnny and Louella were laying in bed, and Louella asked, "Is this what you want Johnny?"

Johnny looked at her, confused, "Yeah, sugah, this is what WE want, isn't it?"

"It seems like a lot of work, and the money is not really all that much. Should we talk to Joshua about booking bigger gigs maybe? Maybe we can do an out of town, if it is on a weekend, or maybe you can take some time off?"

"You were the one who didn't want me to quit my job Louella. You wanted a stable paycheck."

"I still do baby, but let us see what else is out there. Maybe this will go further if we take the risk."

"Do you want me to ask Joshua to book me out of town, or even out of state?"

"I heard there's a few good bars opened in Albany, maybe you can play there? You should ask Joshua if he has contacts in Albany."

"Sugah, Albany is three hours away. How can we get there and back in one night?"

"Talk to Mike. Maybe he can give you the day off, or two, see what we can do, we need to expand if we wanna make it big, if you want to play the Opry."

"OK Sugah, I'll ask, tomorrow, but tonight..." and he reached over and turned off the light.

The next morning, Johnny called his agent.

"Yeah, see what you can do. Yeah, in Albany, make a call, you can? Great, Yeah, I will talk it over with Mike, but I am sure I can get him to agree. Thank You, you are great Joshua."

As Johnny hung up the phone, Louella was at his side looking at him with a smile on her face.

"He said he will make some calls." Johnny said to her unasked question, "But I still gotta run it past Mike. At the best, I still gotta leave work early, and I don't know how this is gonna fly."

"Don't worry about it baby," Louella said, "Mike likes you, and he supports you. I am sure everything will be OK by him."

It took Joshua a couple of days to get back to Johnny with the news.

"You wanted it, my boy, and I delivered." Joshua started, "I got you a one night gig at the Oglethorpe Lounge in Albany."

"That is awesome man!" Johnny said, then covering the receiver he mouthed to Louella, "He got me the Oglethorpe," then turning back to the phone, "So, who am I opening for this time?" Johnny asked.

"That's the cherry on the top, you are the headliner." Joshua told him, "You are getting the reputation. I just mentioned your name and they were practically throwing money at me to get you. You are on the rise my boy."

Johnny covered the receiver again, and said, "I am headlining!" Louella just smiled, and walked over to Johnny and put her arm around his waist, listening to the conversation.

"But," Joshua said to the couple, "It is a Wednesday night. Are you alright with that?"

"I will have to run it past Mike, but I am sure I can make it." Johnny said.

"Got a plan," Joshua said, "Invite him. Tell him that he and Emily will be guest. Full boat . We will pick up you and Louella and him and Emily, bring them down on my bill. Meals and drink, on me. Show him how good you are doing, and even have him bring his guitar."

"Just how much am I getting for this show that we can afford to do this?" Johnny asked.

"You are getting a goodly sum, but don't worry, I am going to foot the extra expense. A gesture of good will." Joshua replied, "Besides, I have a plan."

The next morning Johnny knocked on Mike's door.

"Johnny, come, come in, what can I do for you?"

Johnny looked down at his feet, took a deep breath, then screwed up his courage and said, "Joshua has me booked." looked down at his feet again, then back up to Mike, "At the Oglethorpe Loung."

"Isn't that in Albany?" Mike asked.

"It is, but he wants to do something special for you amd Emily, for all your support."

"Go on." Mike replied.

"He wants you and Em to come, as our guests." Johnny said, feeling a little nervous.

"Guests?" Mike asked.

"Yes. Joshua said that you have been such great supporters, that he wanted to do something special for you, so he is taking the four of us down to Albany, and the whole show is on him. The meal, drinks, he is going to pick us up, take us there, give it the works."

"Sounds very nice, and very expensive. How much are you getting paid for this gig?"

"I am being very well compensated, but Joshua says your tab, is on him, as his gift, for being such a great supporter."

"and when does this 'gift' happen?" Mike asked.

"Next Wednesday." Johnny said, then jerked back a little as if Mike had lashed out at him.

"So you wanna leave early?" Mike said.

"If that is alright with you?: Johnny said, "There is a lot we have to do."

Mike smiled a big, ear to ear smile, then chuckled slightly as he said, "Relax Johnny, I was just giving you the gears. I'll do you one better. Take the day off. Get some rest, maybe have Louella take some time, get her hair done, make her feel special, and where do you want to meet?"

"Joshua says he will pick you and Emily up at home, is that alright?"

"Excellent. Em and I will be ready, say what? Five-ish?"

"That will work, and thank you Mike, I really appreciate this." Johnny said, and turned to leave, then stopped, looked back and said, "Oh, and Joshua says bring your guitar."

"My guitar? Why?"

"Don't know, he just suggested it."

"OK, then." Mike said, "Next Wednesday at five. See you then, but until then, there is a whole truck needs unloading and you're just standing here gawking." and he smiled at Johnny.

It was four in the afternoon when a black limo pulled up in front of Johnny and Louella's apartment, and Joshua stepped out, holding the door open for the couple, who slid onto the seats as Joshua sat across from them.

"Everything changes tonight Johnny." Joshua said, "This is your big break. Louella, lovely dress, is it new?"

"Johnny bought it for me yesterday. Said I needed to look like the wife of a superstar."

"And you do, you look lovely. Johnny?" Joshua said, turning to his protege, "How are you feeling?"

"Nervous as hell." Johnny said.

"Don't be," Joshua said, "Just keep your focus. Focus on being the best fiddler ever, and people will believe it. It is your belief in yourself that makes the magic happen Johnny."

"I can't express how much I appreciate everything you have done for me Joshua. I would never be headlining if it was not for you."

"It is all you my boy. All you. I am just here to make sure you get everything coming to you." then they pulled up in front of Mike and Emily's house, and shortly the couple came out, and climbed into the limo next to Joshua, "Mike," Joshua said, "You didn't bring your guitar?"

"I considered it, but this is Johnny's night, don't want to show the boy up." he smiled at Johnny and slapped him on the knee.

It was a long drive to Albany, Georgia, but the time seemed to fly by as the group chatted about various topics. Johnny's career, Mike's regret he never took the chance to play professionally, and Louella and Emily chatted about various topics of interest to them whenever the guys conversations became boring to them, until finally they arrived at The Oglethorpe Lounge. There was a crowd waiting to get in, and as Johnny stepped out of the limo, everyone in the line cheered. As Johnny and his party moved into the lounge, he shook hands with a few of the people in the line before being ushered into the room. Mike and Emily and Louella were shown their seats as Joshua and Johnny went back stage to get ready for the show.

Johnny took the stage, and started with a frenzied medley of reels before he he introduced himself. Everything he did was letter perfect, and the crowd was crazy for him. He was a three quarters through his set when he finished Orange Blossom Special, then again, addressed the crowd.

"It has been a real pleasure playing for you folks tonight," Johnny started, "but no one get to play here by himself. My manager, Joshua," Johnny pointed his golden bow at his table, and Joshua stood up for the crowd to cheer, "and of course my wife, Louella, who has been with me all the way," and Louella stood and waved to the crowd who cheered as well, "and I would be terribly remiss if I did not include my biggest supporter, and best friend, Mr. Mike Cartwright ladies and gentlemen," and Mike stood up and raised his arms in the air, "but you see, Mike is not just a supporter, he is also a fine musician himself, do you all wanna hear Mike play a little something for you?" and the crowd cheered louder and clapped, "Mike, you git your ass up here buddy, you deserve this." Johnny motioned him up to the stage, and Mike made his way to the stage.

When Mike got up there, he stared out at the crowd and his heart started to pound in his chest. He turned to Johnny and said, "I didn't bring my guitar Johnny, I told you I wasn't gonna steal your time."

Johnny just smiled and made a motion to the side stage area, and one of the technicians came out carrying a guitar and handed it to Mike.

Johnny started playing Beaumont Rag, then paused, and Mike started to play a bit and stopped, then Johnny started again, and Mike joined in until the two of them were playing together and the crowd was cheering the duo. When the song was over, Mike gave the guitar back to Johnny, who turned to the crowd and said, "Mike Cartwright, people, remember that name, one day, you will be able to say you knew him when!" and the crowd cheered as Mike made his way back to table.

When the set was finally done, Johnny joined the group back at the table, and they had a few more drinks, knowing that they were being chauffeured home gave them a bit more leniency in their partying, but soon they knew they had to leave. It was a three hour drive back to Atlanta, and it had already been a very long day. As Johnny shook hands with fans who had stayed behind, and signed autographs, Joshua took Mike aside and said, "I am sorry dude, I did not know Johnny was going to do that. I mean, you didn't even bring a guitar, but to put you on the spot like that, it was not cool. I will talk to him tonight, after we get back to Atlanta. I know he was nervous about headlining, but to try to overshadow you like that, to build himself up at your expense, anyway, I do hope you and Em had a good night, and for what it is worth, you did a very good job for being put upon in such a manner."

Mike shook Joshua's hand, and said, "It was alright. I know I was not all that great, but it was fun, don't mention it to him though, he has too much going on to be bothered with stuff like this."

"You are a good man Mike. I am glad Johnny has a friend like you, who can see past his pettiness, and still see him as a friend. Anyway, let us get you two home." and the limo pulled up next to the party and everyone filed in. The trip back was quieter, and everyone just chalked it up to being late, and tired, but they dropped Mike and Emily off first before taking Johnny and Louella home. Once they got there, Joshua told Louella to go ahead, "I gotta talk to Johnny for a moment, he'll be up in a bit." and Louella smiled, kissed Johnny good night, and said, "Don't be long." and she winked at hm then bounded up the stairs.

"That was incredible!" Johnny said to Joshua, thinking he was going to be congratulated fo the concert.

"Yes yes it was," Joshua said, "You did good, just maybe next time, don't be so quick to share the spolight. t looks bad when people think you need help get through your set."

"I didn't need help." Johnny said, "I was doing Mike a favour."

"That's not the way Mike was telling it" Joshua said, "He told me that it was a good thing you had him there to help you out when you started to get cold feet in the middle there. Just, just don't say anything to him about to Let it go, and it will all blow over, but maybe you might not bring him on stage with you again."

"You can bet hat won't ever happen again." Johnny said, but Joshua took his arm and said, "Let it go Johnny, it isn't worth your friendship."

"Too late." Johnny said and he stalked away to his apartment.

The tension in the warehouse Thursday was palpable. Whether leaning with Mike or with Johnny, no one stayed long, or asked too much. They sensed something was wrong, and no one wanted to get on the wrong side of either by saying something wrong.

That afternoon, Mike looked out his office window and noticed Johnny struggling with a rather awkward box, and felt this would be a good opportunity to smooth over the tension that had developed since last night, and came out on the floor to assist him.

As he put his hands on the box, Mike said, "Here, let me help you." but Johnny turned his body to block him.

"I can do this myself." he said, as he pushed Mike out of the way.

"There is no shame in asking for help Johnny." he said as he tried to reposition himself to get a better grip on the box.

"The day I need help from you is the day I walk out that door!" Johnny said, as he pointed to the exit sign.

"No one is stopping you Johnny. Nothing but your own foolish pride."

"Rather be proud of my own abilities, than jealous of someone else's greatness." Johnny yelled back, and the other warehouse staff, started to notice there were other jobs that had to be done in other parts of the warehouse.

"You think you can make it on your own, Johnny, be my guest." Mike yelled back, and Johnny took a step back, letting go of the box, and allowing it to fall to the ground at Mike's feet.

"I am outta here." he said, and walked to the exit.

"You walk out on your shift Johnny, and don't bother coming back!" Mike shouted across the warehouse, but Johnny just waved a dismissive hand in the air, and walked out the door. Mike looked around at the apparently empty warehouse, then at the box on the floor, and called out, "Anyone feel like working today?" and he turned on his heels back to the office as the warehouse staff came out of hiding and helped put the box back on the shelf.

Louella walked into the apartment after her shift at the bank to find Johnny home, and on the phone.

"All week?" she heard Johnny say into the phone, "Five concerts? Every night? That is great Joshua, I knew you could come through, you are the best man." and as Johnny hung up, he saw Louella standing in the doorway.

"Baby?" she said, "Why are you home so early, and what is this about five concerts?"

"Quit my job sugah." he said as he walked over to Louella, "I am full time now. Me, you, and my golden fiddle. We are going places. Joshua just set me up with a small tour across southern Georgia. All week, 'cept Sunday and Monday. We are hitting Peachtree, Macon, Hinesville, everywhere. This is our big step sugah. "

"But I can't go on tour with you baby." she said," I still have my job, we still need some stability until this so-called big time happens. What about healthcare? What about a steady paycheck? You have five concerts this week, but then what? How many honky-tonks you gotta play? I can't do this."

"Sugah, you know I want you with me all the time, but until I am self sufficient, keep your job. Follow me when you can, but I will always come back to you sugah, you know that."

"I do Johnny," she said, "but it still scares me. Things are going so fast, but I trust you. Go. Be famous, and I will be here when you get back." then she kissed him, and said, "But until then, someone still has to make supper." and she hung up her coat and went to the kitchen.

Tuesday, Johnny kissed Louella good bye as she left for the bank, and by the afternoon, He and Joshua were in a minivan that Joshua leased for the micro tour. It was the most economical method of transportation and the gigs Joshua booked were paying more than the other small venues he had played in Atlanta, so even with the motel rooms, meals and transportation, he still came home with a large amount of cash.

Louella came home from shopping for dinner to find Johnny home, sitting in the their little living room with Joshua and she flung herself at him.

"Baby, I have missed you so much." she said as she threw her arms around his next as he stood to greet her.

"I have missed you too sugah." he said, "But I am home for now, and, I come bearing gifts." and he reached for the table and took a rectangular felt box, and as he opened it, he said, "For all you have put up with." and he opened the box to reveal a shimmering silver tennis bracelet.

"Oh baby!" she cried, literally, as tears flowed down her cheek, "Are, are these diamonds?" and her eyes were like saucers.

"Swarovski Crystals." Joshua said, knowing Johnny would not be able to pronounce the name.

"What he said." Johnny added, "But one day, one day you will be draped in diamonds." Louella hugged him tighter and kissed him with all her passion until Joshua just kind of backed out of the room and as he closed the apartment door, he mouth "I'll call you." and Johnny gave him the Thumbs Up as his mouth was currently very preoccupied.

Sunday afternoon the phone rang. Johnny answered the phone as Louella made some sweet tea. From the kitchen she could hear part of Johnny's side of the conversation.

"Hmm, mm, yeah. How long? The whole south? Festivals? Hmm, mmm, sure, I mean it's a long time, but yeah, sure, thanks Joshua." and as he hung up the phone Louella walked in with the pitcher of sweet tea.

"What did Joshua say this time, baby?" and as she put the pitcher down, she looked into his eyes, "Another show?"

"Shows, sugah." Johnny said, "Shows, plural. There are all kinds of festivals going on in the south, and Joshua wants to hit as many as we can. This will be the whole summer sugah. All across the south. Kentucky, Tennessee, Arkansas, everywhere, this can mean big money for us sugah."

"I might be able to get a couple of weeks baby," Louella said, "But the whole summer? I don't think I can do that. Last week was torture. Not being with you."

"Talk to your boss. Come with me for part of the tour, but you don't have to come to all the shows, and I will be back, you know I will."

Johnny and Louella spent the week together as Joshua lined up all the acts Johnny was to play, and the following Monday, she kissed him goodbye and watched him load up the minivan and drive off into the distance. She was sad, since she was not able to be with him at the beginning of the tour, but she was going to make sure she could meet up with by the end of the tour.

The first week was amazing, and Johnny and Joshua were hitting a different city every night. Johnny would make sure he called Louella each night before he went on. Hearing her voice made the loneliness seem smaller, but by the second week, Johnny had some midday gigs, and sometimes did not have the time to call, but he always tried to follow it up the next day if he missed one night, but soon, people were inviting him to restaurants, taking him out after shows, and time started to slip from him. Sunday night, of his third week on the road, he was sitting in his motel room talking to Louella since he had missed calling her for two days straight, and he was starting to feel lonely. Joshua, who at the start, was with him for every show, was seldom around anymore, as he had other clients to take care of, and the endless travel was starting to wear on him when there was a knock on his door.

"Sugah, I have to go, I think my dinner just arrived. Love you."

"Love you too, baby." she said, and he hung up the phone and opened the door. A young brunette in a long coat and high heels stood in his doorway.

"Can I, can, can I help you miss?" Johnny stammered. The woman smiled, stepped into the room, and shut the door behind her. As soon as the lock clicked, she dropped her coat to reveal she was only wearing lingerie.

The next morning Johnny woke to the naked body of the woman who came to him last night. Guilt hit him. How could he do this? Why? He felt ashamed, but at the same time, all the pent up frustration and loneliness was gone. Johnny showered, dressed and packed his things, and left the unknown woman in the bed, trying to pretend last night didn't happen. The next night, still shaken from his slip, he spent the whole day locked in his motel until his show, moved to the theatre, did his act, and left to go back to his room, watching everywhere to make sure there wasn't another trench coat clad woman waiting to move on him. Joshua showed up Wednesday night to check on him, and make sure he was being treated well. Johnny told him he was having a blast, but even between guys, he did not really want to let slip his indiscretion. Joshua hung around a couple of days, then said his goodbyes and left Johnny with the parting words, "Have fun, and don't do anything I wouldn't do." then laughing he drove away.

About the fifth weekend of his tour, Johnny was playing a festival of fiddle and bluegrass, and meeting many great and famous fiddle players, people he idolized all his life and was in awe of being in the presence of so many huge names, and even many talented up and comers. One act that caught his attention was a sister trio, who all played fiddle, each one with a unique style of their own that complimented each other. Johnny was mainstage that night, second to last act, but the sisters were a fill in just before his act, and when he was done, to an incredibly thunderous ovation, he was feeling very excited, and charged. He had to call Louella, who answered n the first ring.

"Oh my god Louella!" he shouted into the phone, so pumped, "That was the most amazing set I have ever played. The electricity the air is incredible. I just wish you could be here tonight. I so wish I could share this night with you."

"Do you Johnny?" Louella smiled as she spoke into her cell phone, "Are you sure you want me there? I won't cramp your style?"

Johnny felt a small pang of guilt about the brunette, but that was weeks ago, so he swallowed hard, put on a smile, and said, No sugah you know I love you. If you could be here tonight, I would show you just how much I love you."

"I love you to baby." she said, then she closed her phone, and smiled at Joshua.

"See, I told you he misses you" Joshua said to her, then, "Now, his act just finished, there will be one more act, then he will probably head to his room. e should be there in about ninety minutes, are you alright to do this?"

"I am. Louella said, and climbed into Joshua's car as he drove her to Johnny's motel room.

After the show, the sisters walked up to Johnny.

"You play a mighty find fiddle boy." the eldest sister said, "Would you like to show us a little of your famed" and she winked at Jonny as she said, "fingering?"

Johnny looked at the girls, then talking to the eldest sister said, "Sure, I can show you some work."

The sisters looked at each other and smiled then the spokeswoman said, "No, I don't want you to show me, WE, and she gestured to her two sisters and herself, "want you to show US,"a nd she leaned close to Johnny's ear so that her breath tickled the hair s on his neck, "What you can do"

Johnny stepped back and looked at the three women. Each was strikingly beautiful, with jet black hair, pale skin and a shockingly deep red lipstick. Each was dressed in a long gown, the two younger sisters in red and their elder sibling in black. Johnny looked around, and since the show was shutting down for the night his pal got sweaty, but then he just looked into their eyes and nodded. Johnny brought them to his minivan, and the two younger sisters crawled into the back, and the elder sat in the front next to Johnny and they all rode to his motel room.

Once in the room, the sisters dropped all pretense of wanting fiddle lessons and proceeded to fulfill any and all fantasies Johnny might have had. He was still high from giving such an incredible performance, and so full of raw energy that how wrong what he was doing never crossed his mind at all, he was lost in his own lust. Finally, the sisters turned off the lights and they all gave in to their desires.

Joshua came out of the motel office with a spare key to Johnny's room.

"How did you get that?" Louella sked

"I can be particularly persuasive." Joshua said.

"I guess that comes in handy being an agent." she said as Joshua stopped in front of Johnny's room and handed Louella they key.

Joshua kissed the top of her head and said, "Don't do anything I wouldn't do." and left her alone in front of the motel room. Louella pulled open the front of her coat and looked at the somewhat form fitting dressed she was wearing, took a deep breath, slid the key into the door, and walked into the room. The room was very dark, smelled of sweat, and the soft moans and cries of women came to her, and she immediately flipped on the light switch, bathing Johnny and the three sisters in fluorescent light, their pale skin glistening with sweat, their hair matted to their faces, and her husband, laying spread eagle on the bed surrounded by these women. Louella said nothing, felt, nothing, she just turned on her heels and stormed out of the room as Johnny struggled to free himself from the sisters and run after his wife. By the time he made it to the door, all he could see was a pair of taillights disappearing into the night.

"Come back to bed Johnny." the three sisters chimed, but Johnny didn't hear them. He was too upset, too angry at his actions. What had he done? Why did he do it? What compelled him to be so utterly stupid? When he felt the eldest sister wrapped her arms around his waist and pulled him against her body he suddenly realized they were still here, and his anger flared.

"Get Out!" he shouted and pointed to the open door as he stood in the center and the sisters hastily slipped into their dresses, ignoring any lingerie they might have left behind, climbed into a cherry red Trans Am, which Johnny could have sworn wasn't there when he arrived in his minivan, but at the moment didn't mean anything. He just sat on the edge of the bed and cried.

The next day Joshua called Johnny.

"Johnny!" he said, his voice full of concern, "What the hell happened?"

"Louella." Johnny said, Louella came here last night."

"I know, I drove her. She wanted to surprise you. She got the week off. She asked me to take her to you. She wanted to be with you, then the next thing I know, she is climbing back into my car and crying, sobbing 'take me home. Take me home'. What happed man?"

"I fucked up man. I met these girls, these sisters, and I was so hyped from my performance, and they were so willing, and I never thought, I mean, she never said anything, I was just so high on adrenaline. It's no excuse, and I shouldn't have done it, but I have been so lonely, and, and..."

"Don't worry Johnny, I will fix everything, you, you just finish the tour man. I will talk to Louella, I will fix this for you, I will, just, and I really cannot express this enough Johnny ... KEEP IT IN YOUR PANTS." I can fix this for you, but you have to stop doing this."

"Doing what?" Johnny asked, confused, "This is the first time anything like this has ..."

"Yes, Johnny, like when you fiddle, believe it, and it will happen, you keep telling yourself it was only one time, the other girl, never happened."

Before Johnny could get Joshua to explain how he knew about the other girl, Joshua was gone.

Every day, Johnny would sit in his room until it was show time. He would rush to the stage, play his music, the crowds would roar, then he would pack up and leave, never sticking around for autographs, or to meet with fans, he would just go back to his room and call Louella, who never answered.

For the next two weeks Johnny kept to his routine, which at some of the smaller venues, where it was just him, and some opening acts, or the main act, if he was an opener, were easier, but his brusque attitude was starting to grate on some people. The festivals, even the small ones, were harder. He usually had to stay around for various sessions, and there was seldom any place for him to hide, and the adoring fans clamoring for his autograph conflicted him. He so much needed to connect with his fans, but he was finding it hard to fight off his desires. The longer he was away from Louella, the lonelier he was, and the more need for intimate contact kept scratching at him.

In his last week of the tour, Joshua stopped by to check on him. He found Johnny in his dressing room, his golden fiddle laying on the cot he rested on, and Johnny sitting in a chair crying.

"Listen, Johnny," Joshua said, "Pull yourself together. The tour is almost over. You can go home, but you have to get through this show tonight, and for god's sake, don't go scurrying away after the show. Stay. Schmooze. Talk to people."

Johnny looked at his manager through bloodshot eyes, took a deep breath, and tried to force a smile.

"See," Joshua said, "Like that. Just smile, breathe, relax. You can get through this, you can do this."

Joshua left Johnny on his own until his set was due, and Johnny just sat in his room trying to calm himself, when there was a knock on the door.

"Johnny?" a small voice came from behind the door but Johnny just ignored it.

"Johnny?" the voice said again, and then the door slowly opened and a young girl carrying an autograph book, poked her head in.

"Johnny, is it, is, is it, is it OK if I get your autograph?"

Johnny looked up at the girl, and tried to smile, which was rather easy because she was a very cute girl, and he just wanted to smile. "Sorry, " and he paused, waiting for her to say her name.

"Lise." she said, "My name is Lise."

"Lise." he said, more to himself, than to her, "That is a nice name, but I have to go on soon. Maybe later? After the show? Will that be alright?"

Lise beamed at him, "Why yes, after, but not too late, my mommy is picking me up after the show, but I can come back quickly, if you like."

"That would be wonderful, Lise." Johnny said, then shooed her away from the door, and Lise skipped down the hallway to her seat.

Lise had barely left the room when Joshua poked his head in the room, backed out a moment to look down the hall, then looked back at Johnny.

"5 minutes Johnny. You ready to go on?" he said.

Johnny nodded, then picked up his golden fiddle, and walked to the door. Joshua stopped him just before he left, and said, "Remember, focus on what you want, believe it, and it will happen." then again looking down the hallway, he said, "In all things, not just your music." Johnny nodded again, and walked past Joshua.

That night, Johnny gave the performance of his career. Every song perfect. Every note on key. Songs he heard, but never played before were flowing from him on a whim. He just focused on the songs he wanted to play, and they came to him, flowing from his golden fiddle and capturing the crowd, and the crowd was soaking it all up. Finally, Johnny looked out over the crowd, and somehow, in some manner he did not understand, he could see Lise sitting way in the back row.

"The road is a long and lonely trek." he said to the audience, "There is not a lot of time to make friends, so when you find one, keep her." and it was like Lise was lit up by the house lights in a sea of shadow, "So this one, is for that special friend we meet along the road of life, and I hope you like it." and Johnny began to play, and somehow, Lise knew the song was for her, and her heart started pounding, and her palms were sweaty. Johnny was playing a song just for her.

Like the night at the festival, Johnny was again feeling incredibly elated by his performance. His body was vibrating with excitement, and he was finding it hard to come down. He paced in his dressing room. Lay on his cot. Paced again. He could not seem to stop moving when there was a knock on his door.

"Johnny?" Joshua called in as he slowly opened the door, "You alright?"

"Yes, yes, I am alright, quite right, yes." Johnny said in rapid succession.

"Good, I have a fan here to see you, are you good to receive visitors?"

Johnny practically leapt across the room to the door and swung it open, almost pulling Joshua into the room with him, and there, in his doorway, was Lise.

"Lise!" Johnny said, his voice high with excitement, "Lise, yes, autograph, yes, come in dear, come in, Joshua, thank you, you can go, thank you." and he pulled Lise into the room and pushed the door closed as Joshua said, "I will be back later, Johnny. Don't do anything I wouldn't do." and with that, the door clicked shut.

Lise held out her book, and a pen and smiled at Johnny.

"Did you like the concert Lise?" Johnny asked.

"It was amazing Johnny." she said, "At the end, that song, it felt like you were only singing it to me."

"Did you like that Lise? Did you like thinking the song was only for you?" and Lise smiled and nodded, her head bobbing like a paint shaker as she continued to hold out the autograph book and pen. Johnny took the book and pen from her and place it on the table.

"Come here Lise." he said as he held his arms out to her, and Lise walked slowly toward him, watching him carefully. "Come, Lise, gimme a hug." he said, and scooped her up in his arms.

"My mom is waiting," she said, trying to pull away.

"I know, do you want me to play you a song?" Johnny asked as he picked up his golden fiddle, "One song? Before you go?" and he released her from the hug. Lise smiled at him, and nodded, then sat in one of the chairs, and asked, "Then I will get my autograph?"

Johnny pulled the bow across his golden fiddle and it made an evil hiss as he said, "Yes, you will my friend." and he started to play.

Lise sat in the chair and listened to the music, swaying a little.

"You like this?" Johnny asked, and Lise nodded, "Do you want to dance for me Lise?" and Lise rose from her chair and started to sway to the music. As she danced, her movements became more animated, and Johnny smiled at her, and said, "You can dance better without your clothes." and Lise's brow crinkled, but Johnny played a little faster, and Lise danced faster, and the smile returned.

20 minutes later, Joshua was knocking at Johnny's door again, then opened it. "Johnny?" he called into the room, "Lise? Lise? Your mother is here." and he stepped into the room to find Lise sobbing on the edge of the cot.

"Johnny!" Joshua whisper-yelled, "What have you done?"

"Lise and I had a good time. I played her a song, and she showed me her appreciation." Johnny said as Joshua pulled Lise up from the cot and put his arm around her.

"We have to talk Johnny." Joshua said, "Once I try to smooth THIS over." and he started to take Lise out of the room.

"Wait, Lise." Johnny said, as he wrote, Lise, Thanks for everything, Johnny, in her book, which she grabbed from him as Joshua led her out the door.

A few days later, his tour was over, and Joshua managed to keep everything under wraps, from the press, from Louella, and from the police. He still booked Johnny in many different venues, and he was away from home for extended periods of time. Their marriage was stressed, and even though Johnny promised he was faithful, absolute trust was broken. Johnny's fame was changing him. His wealth grew, but his skill was such that he no longer felt he required practice. He slept most of the day when on tour. He started hiring people to load his van, set up his gear, and do everything for him as he sat around and barked orders.

He made sure Joshua booked Mondays and Tuesdays off from performing so he could spend time with Louella, and when he came home, he always brought her a present, took her to expensive restaurants, made passionate love to her each night, then Wednesday morning, he would be gone again and Louella would be all alone.

In the spring, about nine months since Johnny had found his golden fiddle, he and Louella were moving into their new house. Louella still had her job at the bank, and she was adamant she would never leave. She felt someone needed to be grounded. Needed to remember where they came from, even while sitting on five acres of real-estate. In the basement was a largely unfinished section.

"Do you think this would be a great place to build a recording studio?" Louella asked, "If you had a studio, you could make albums, then you wouldn't have to tour all the time. People could listen to you whenever they wanted."

"Joshua and the roadies are coming over for the house warming, I'll ask him about a record deal."

"That would be wonderful baby." Louella said, "I miss you so much when you are away, and then you are only back for a few days then you leave me again, and in this," and Louella made a sweeping gesture to take in the whole area, "Will just seem more empty without you."

The party raged all night. The roadies rubbed elbows with prominent club owners, and promoters. Neighbours, invited as a sign of welcome, and so they wouldn't have the party shut down enjoyed meeting the great Johnny, and listened to him play his golden fiddle. The morning sun warmed the sleeping bodies scrawled across the grounds and the smell of breakfast cooking roused more people. Joshua dug himself out from under two women whom he didn't even recognize, and walked over to Johnny cooking bacon on the barbeque.

"Joshua!" Johnny called out, waving a bottle of Jim Beam, "Hair of the Dog?" he said before taking a swig from the bottle, "And, I got a favour to ask." as Joshua lurched his way over to the grill.

"Want do you need Johnny?" he asked as he looked around and checked his pockets, "Where's my tie?" and Johnny pointed over to one of the women Joshua crawled out from under and saw her tied to the bench with his tie.

"You went all 50 shades on Becky." Johnny laughed, then said, "So, how are you at getting me a record deal? And maybe setting up a home studio?"

"What do you say we table that until after the Memorial Day weekend?" Joshua said.

"Why?" Johnny asked, then shouted over his shoulder, "First batch done Louella!, More pig!" and Louella came in with a plate of fresh bacon, and a plate to take away the cooked bacon.

"Hey Joshua," she said, then looking past him, said, "Sleep well?"

"Hey Sugah," Johnny said, "Joshua says he can set me up with a record deal, AFTER the memorial day weekend."

"Why?" Louella asked, and they both looked at Joshua with questions in their eyes.

"I booked you the Opry the Memorial Day weekend." Joshua said, and Louella dropped her plate of cooked bacon and Johnny dropped his whiskey bottle.

"No Shit!" the two said in unison, "The Opry!?"

"I said I would have you in the Opry within a year. I am four months ahead of schedule." Joshua smiled.

"Well, I have to make more bacon," Johnny said, "Louella has more eggs and pancakes to make, and," looking past Joshua again, "Felicity is untying Becks, I think she wants a turn." then, patting Joshua on the shoulder, he moved toward the impromptu stage they set up last night and shouted enough to wake everyone, who had yet to rise, "I'm going to the OPRY!"

Johnny had no idea how much went into performing at the Opry. His typical slothful demeanor was pushed away as setups, and rehearsals plagued his days. His "I Don't Need To Rehearse." attitude was not tolerated and he had not a moment rest as everything was happening all around him, but through it all, he looked off to the side stage, and there was always Louella, who was granted time off from the bank because this was a hallmark moment in her husband's career.

Unfortunately, Johnny wasn't opening, or closing, he was just one of the many performers scheduled for that night, but the disappointment in not being top billing was over shadowed by the fact that he was actually playing The Grande Ole Opry, and that alone was worth the shot to his pride.

"Ladies and Gentlemen!" the announcer barked out, as Louella straightened Johnny's tie, and straightened the shoulders of his jacket, "Give it up for the man with the golden fiddle, all the way from Atlanta Georgia, and his first ever time at the Opry ... JOHNNY!" and the crowd went crazy, and suddenly, the fact that he was not top bill didn't mean anything, these were his people, his fans, and this was why he was here.

Johnny opened with 'The Devil Went Down to Georgia' with garnered a mix of applause and laughs at the joke, then a medley of bluegrass tunes, and some more contemporary fiddle music. After that, he took a pause to address the audience, and give a speech about the veterans and their sacrifices when a sudden murmur came from the crowd as two men walked onto the stage and approached him. With the microphone still on, they said, "Johnathan Willby Rasmuth, you are under arrest for the statutory rape of one Lise Olivose, a sixteen year old minor you engaged in intercourse with in your dressing room. You have the right to remain silent. If you give up that right, anything you say can and will be held against you in a court of law. You have ...." and soon the words were just droning in his ears and he was handcuffed and dragged off the stage to a series of gasps from the audience, and pleas from Louella as they took him away, and he recalled Louella saying something about getting Joshua.

Johnny sat behind the glass in his orange jumpsuit, and talked into the phone to Joshua.

"I thought you took care of this Joshua. You said you would handle it."

"I did, Johnny," Joshua said, "Until the girl showed up pregnant. Don't you read romance books? You have unprotected sex with a virgin and she will get pregnant. It's a trope that you fell into. I got you out of everything else, but you knock up a minor, and people are going to find out."

"You did this to me. Everything. This is all your doing." Johnny was yelling into the phone until the guards started to move toward him.

"No Johnny, you did this. I was the brunette. I was the three sisters. I was all the little one night stands you had on the way, but YOU were the one who wanted sex with a minor, that is all on you. That is YOUR PRIDE. Your belief that you could do anything you wanted because of the skill of your devil-spawned fiddle. It was all you Johnny. You who thought you could get away with it, could get away with anything, even beating ME." and Joshua hung up the phone and walked away.

# Steve Thorne

S teve Thorne lives in a little town called Edmonton, in Northern Alberta, Canada, and has had an interest in writing since grade school. Since Life is what happens when you are busy making plans, a lot of his dreams went unfulfilled, until now.

Printed in Great Britain
by Amazon